Chapter One

The entire world seemed to stand still. Shen Long, the dragon god, floated in the air, so huge that he blotted out the sky. Magic crackled from his body like lightning. In the moonlight, his great, hulking form cast a deep shadow that nearly erased Emperor Pilaf and his assistants Shu and Mai.

"Un-unbelievable," Pilaf breathed. Shu and Mai nodded in agreement.

Just beyond the shadow, Oolong and Pu'ar stood frozen in terror. Moments before, they had escaped Pilaf's dungeon, hoping to stop the evil emperor from assembling the Dragon Balls and summoning Shen Long. But they were too late. Now, it seemed, there was nothing they could do but watch the dragon grant Pilaf's wish.

Suddenly, a voice like rolling thunder filled the air. "Think well upon your wish, mortal," the dragon god roared at Pilaf. "For although I will grant *any* wish, I will grant only *one*."

"Right," Pilaf stammered. "One wish. Got it."

From deep inside Pilaf's castle, Goku watched the scene unfold. "Wow!" he cried. "A real dragon! And it's *huge!*"

"Well, at least *someone* got his wish," Bulma snapped. All Goku had wanted from the beginning of their quest was to see Shen Long, and here he was.

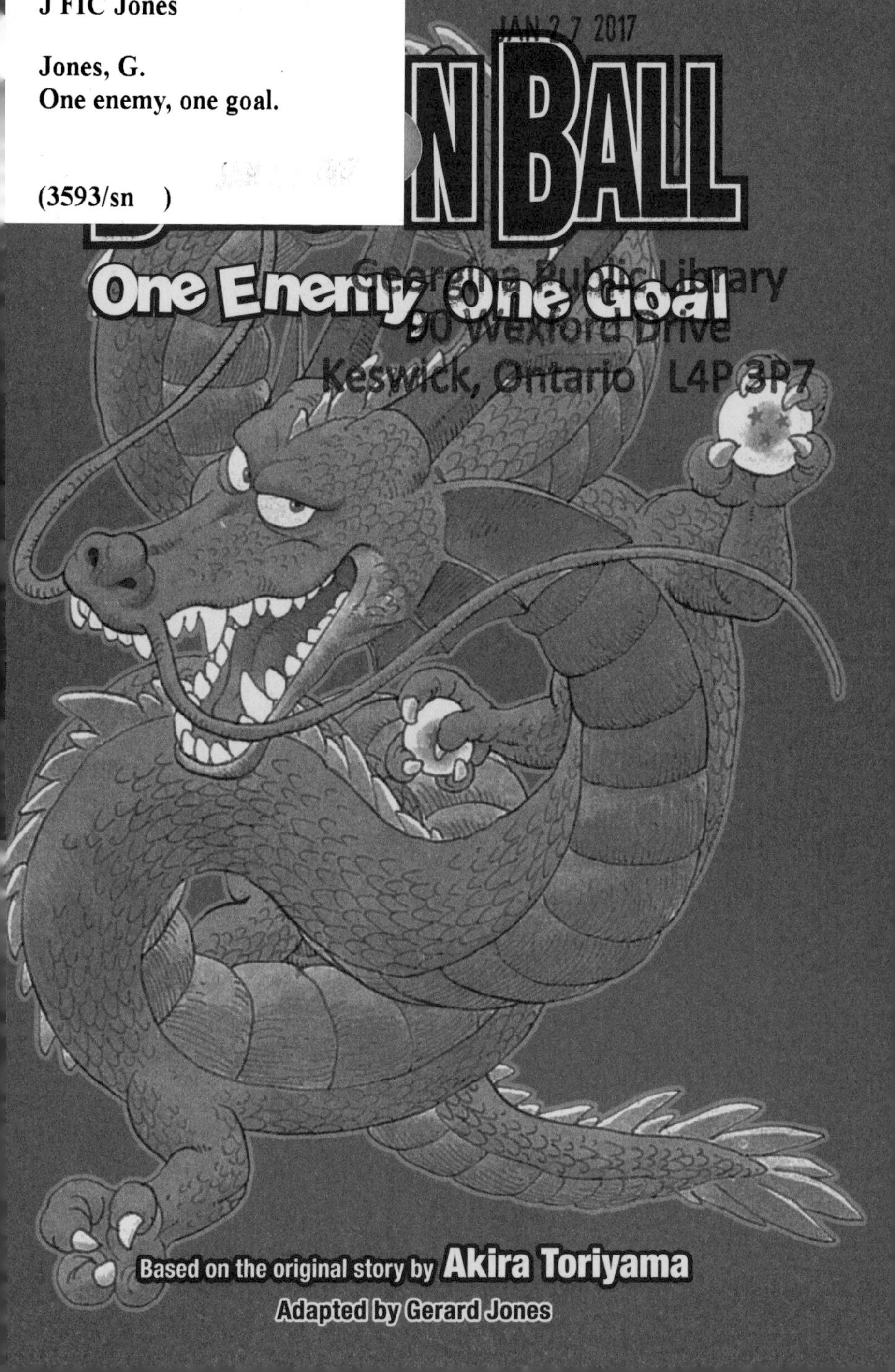

One Enemy, One Goal
Based on the original story by Akira Toriyama
Adapted by Gerard Jones

DRAGON BALL ONE ENEMY, ONE GOAL
CHAPTER BOOK 5

Illustrations: Akira Toriyama
Design: Frances O. Liddell
Coloring: ASTROIMPACT, Inc.
Touch-Up: Frances O. Liddell & Walden Wong
Original Story: Akira Toriyama
Adaptation: Gerard Jones

The stories, characters and incidents mentioned in this publication are
entirely fictional.

Sources for page 78, "A Note About Shen Long":

Giddens, Owen. *Chinese Mythology.* New York: The Rosen Publishing Group, 2006.

Wikipedia contributors, "Shenlong," *Wikipedia, The Free Encyclopedia,* http://en.wikipedia.org/wiki/Shenlong
(Accessed June 19, 2009).

Printed in the U.S.A.

Published by
VIZ Media, LLC
P.O. Box 77010
San Francisco, CA 94107

10 9 8 7 6 5 4 3 2 1
First printing, November 2009

www.vizkids.com   www.viz.com

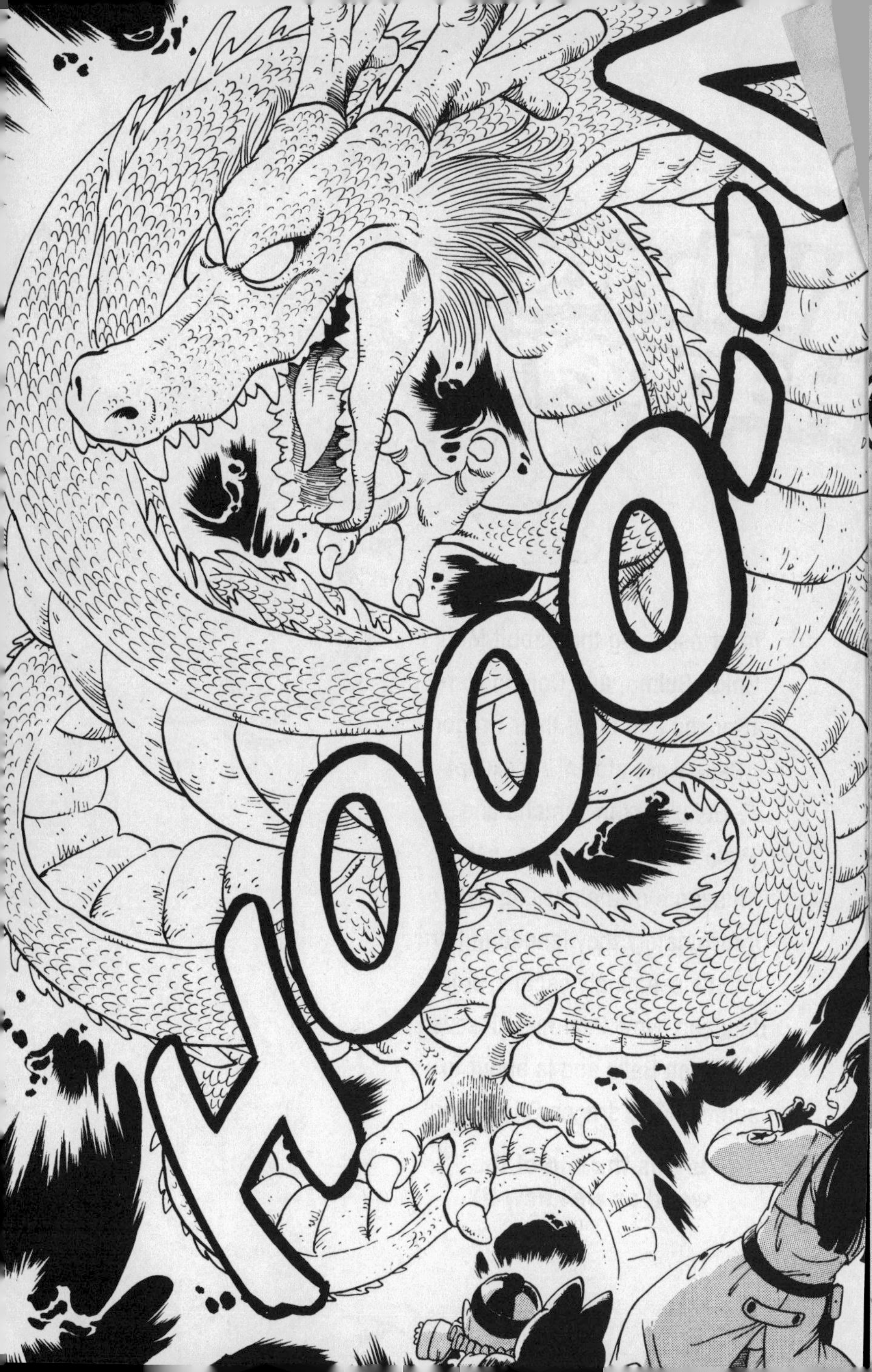
YOOOO!

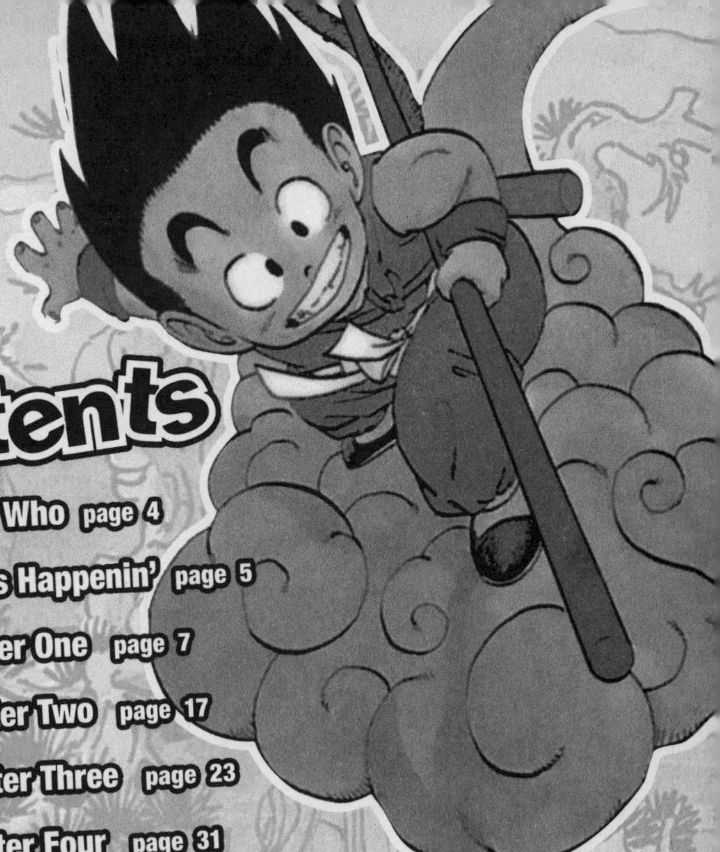

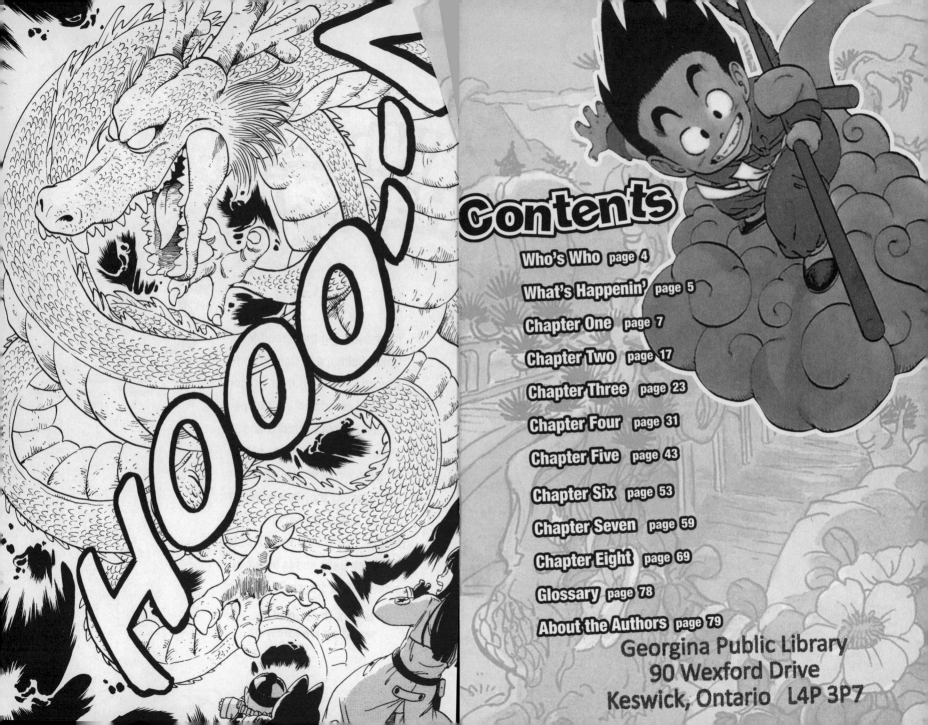

Contents

Who's Who

Bulma
Bulma's from the wide world and is a technological genius. She's also a little hung up on her looks, but nobody's perfect. Besides, without her Goku'd still be hanging out in the forest, catching fish with his tail.

Goku
Since the death of his grandfather, Goku has lived alone, deep in a forest completely cut off from the wide world. He's small for his age but unnaturally strong. And what's with that tail?

Oolong
Can you count on this shifty little piggie? Not by the hair on your chinny-chin-chin!

Pu'ar

Pu'ar is Yamcha's shape-shifting sidekick.

Yamcha
Yamcha thinks he's the king hyena in a land of scavengers, but his bark is a lot worse than his bite.

Pilaf

He's small and not too bright, but he might just bumble into world domination.

Mai and Shu

One could say they're the brains behind Pilaf's whole operation. But one wouldn't say that to Pilaf.

Shen Long

The wish-granting dragon only appears when all seven Dragon Balls are brought together.

What's Happenin'

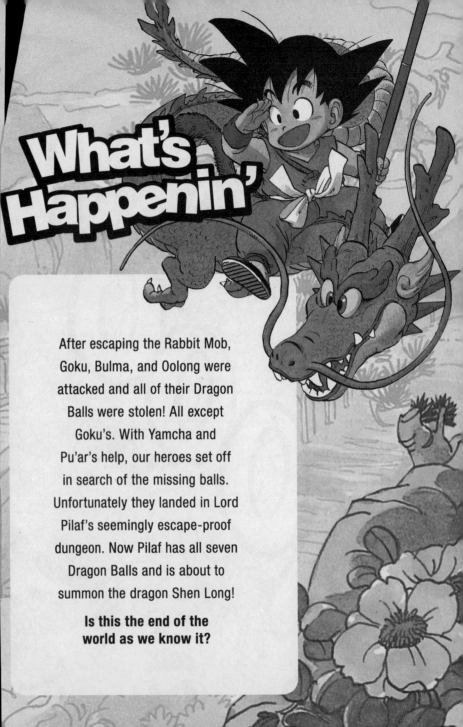

After escaping the Rabbit Mob, Goku, Bulma, and Oolong were attacked and all of their Dragon Balls were stolen! All except Goku's. With Yamcha and Pu'ar's help, our heroes set off in search of the missing balls. Unfortunately they landed in Lord Pilaf's seemingly escape-proof dungeon. Now Pilaf has all seven Dragon Balls and is about to summon the dragon Shen Long!

Is this the end of the world as we know it?

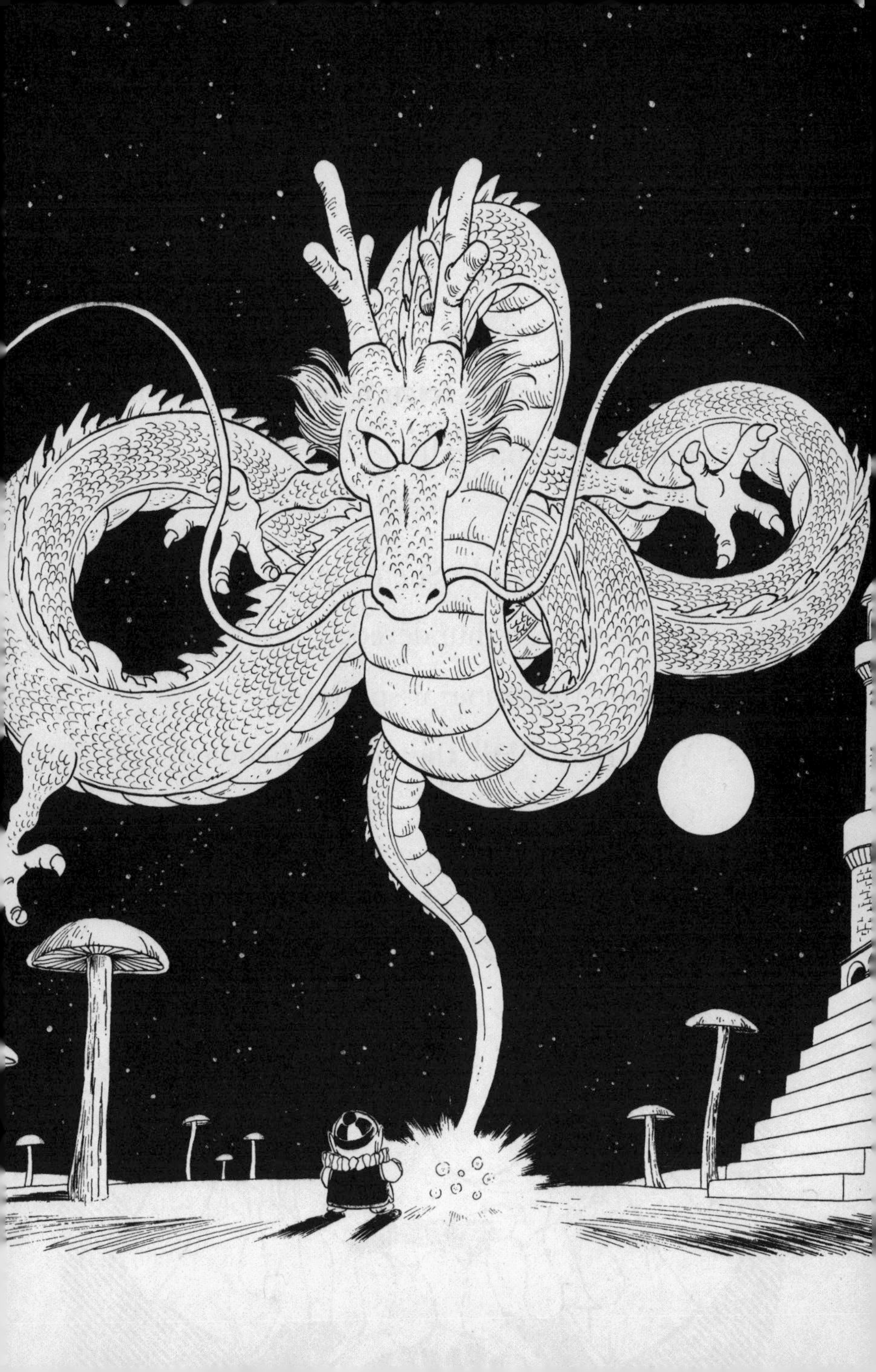

"I was so close!" she whined. "If King Weirdo hadn't stolen my Dragon Balls *I'd* be out there making *my* wish!"

But instead, she, Goku, and Yamcha were trapped in Pilaf's dungeon, forced to watch the emperor and the dragon from a small hole Goku had blasted in the prison wall.

Outside the castle Shen Long was growing impatient. "Well?" he thundered.

"Y-yes?" the emperor sputtered.

"YOUR WISH!" the dragon boomed.

"Oh! Yes! Right!"

Pilaf closed his eyes. He knew exactly what he wanted to wish for. It was the only thing he had ever wanted: to rule the entire world. All he had to do was say the words. "Okay," he said, taking a deep breath. "Here goes..."

"Something tells me this would be a good time to disappear," Oolong said.

"Something's telling me the same thing," Pu'ar agreed.

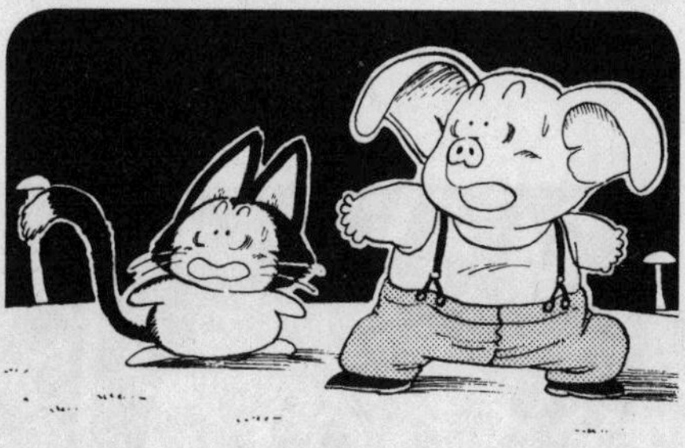

But just as he was about to run, Oolong had an idea. After a moment, the idea became a plan. A plan that would require him to be brave, and that wasn't a very Oolong thing to be. But for some reason–perhaps because the moon was full, the stars were bright, and life as he knew it was about to end–the pig forgot his fear. Without a word, he raced toward

Shen Long as fast as his little legs could take him.

"I wish," Pilaf said again, pronouncing each word carefully so there was no chance the dragon would misunderstand him. "I...wish...for..."

"UNDERPANTS!" Oolong cried breathlessly, arriving just in time. "CLEAN UNDERPANTS!"

Once again time seemed to stop. Pilaf, Shu, and Mai all turned and gaped at the pig. From their cell, Goku, Bulma, and Yamcha couldn't believe their ears.

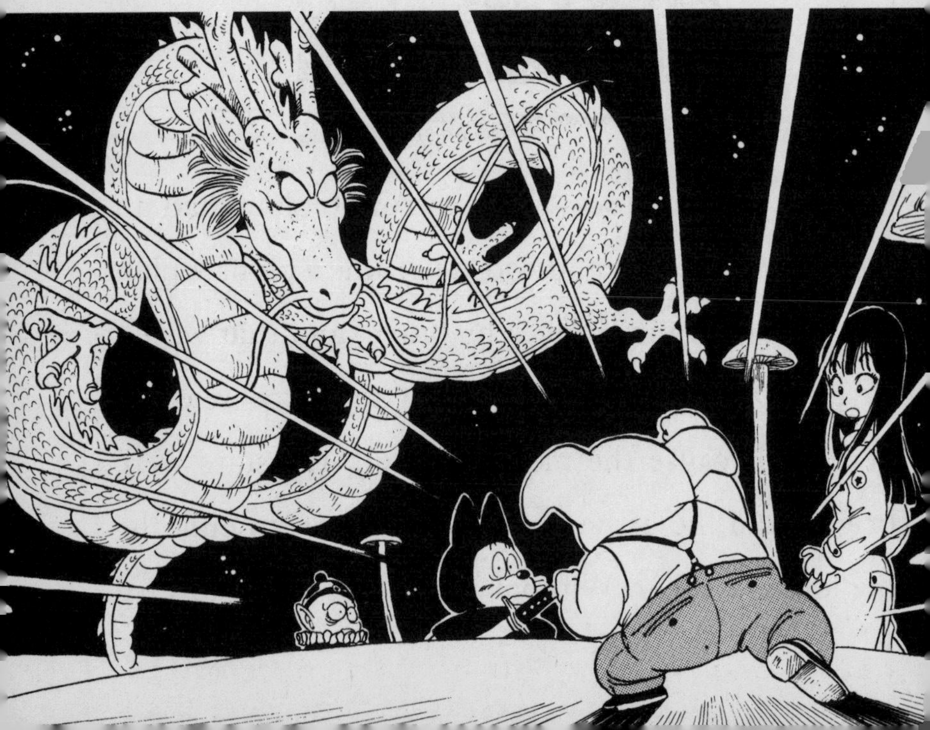

Suddenly, a flash of light split the sky. A BOOM louder than the loudest thunder ripped through the air.

Then something small and white appeared among the stars. It drifted slowly down, down, down…until it landed with a soft FUMP on Oolong's face.

"Ahh," Oolong sighed, pulling the thing from his face. "April fresh. Only…they're a bit small…"

"Your wish is granted," Shen Long rumbled. "Fare thee well."

WHAT?!" Pilaf screamed. "But...but...I'm the one who gathered the Dragon Balls! I'm the one who summoned you!

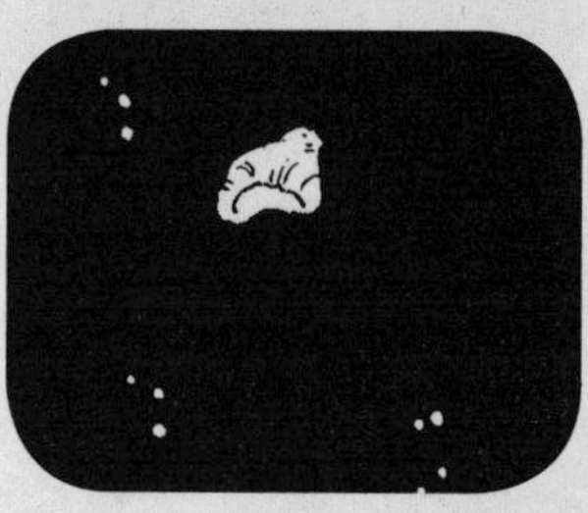

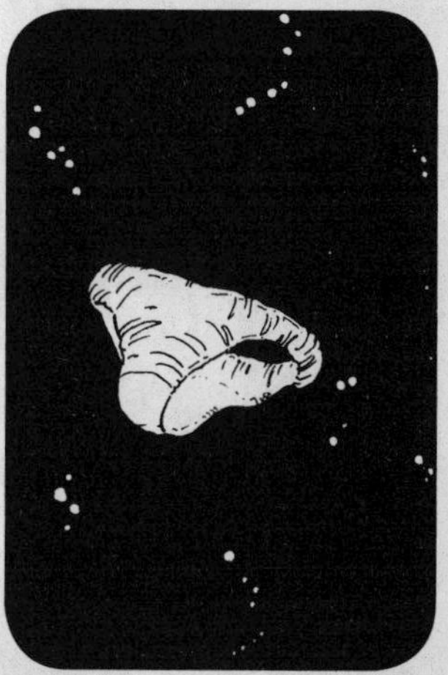

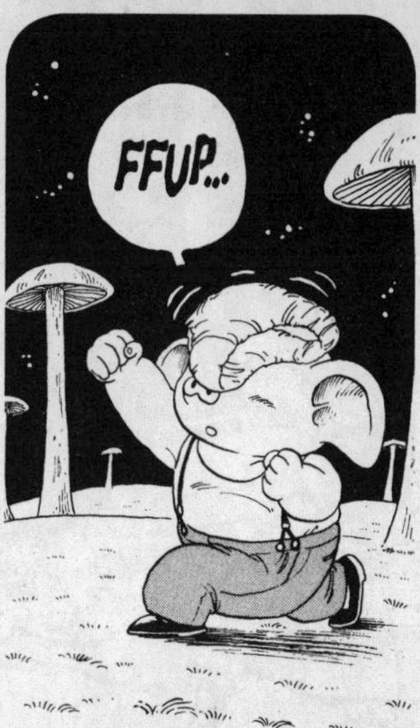
FFUP...

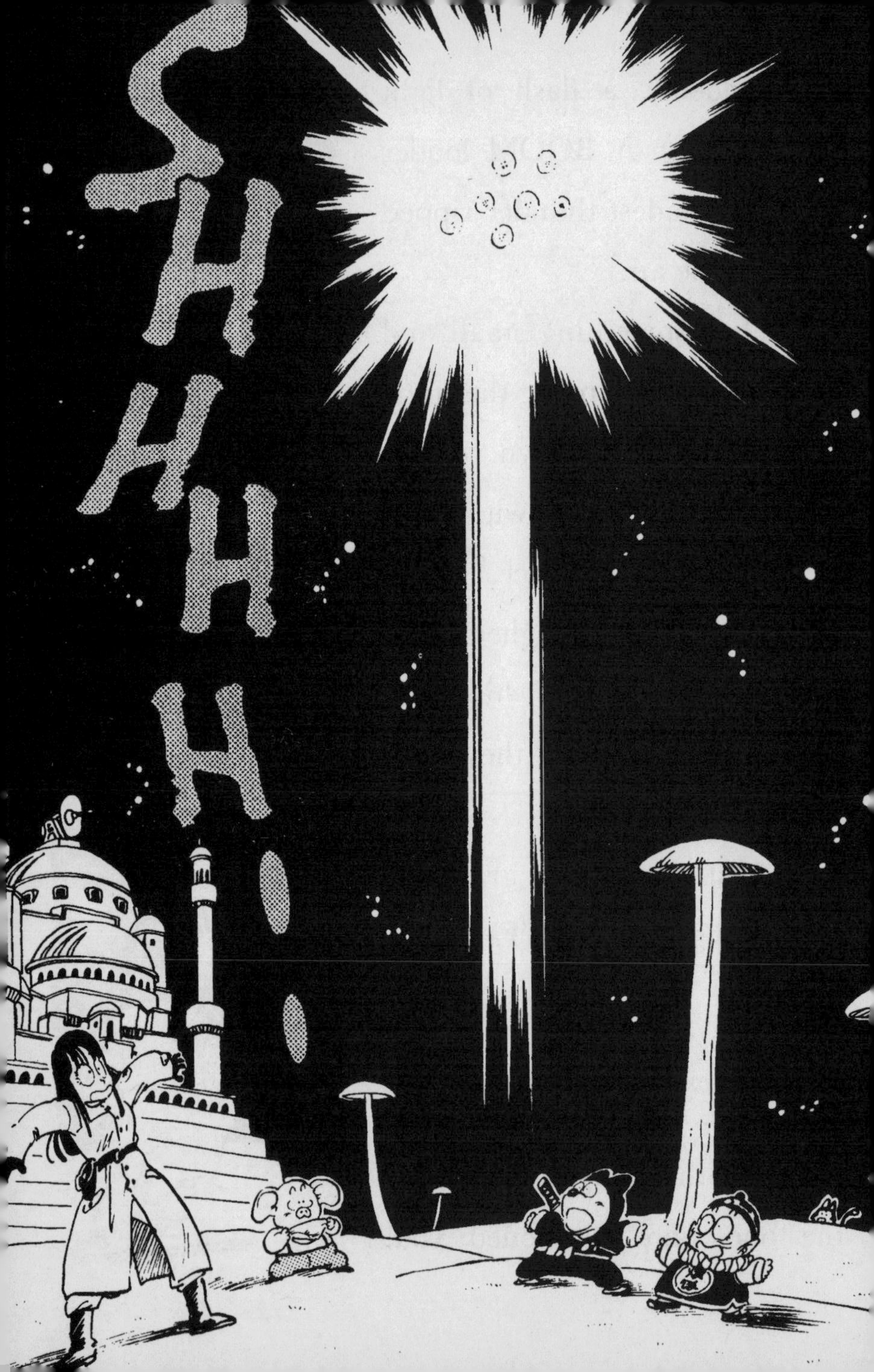
SHHHH!!

I'm the one who deserves the wish! And what I wish for is to rule—"

POOF! Pilaf found himself screaming at nothing but stars and the rising moon. The dragon god had vanished.

In the same instant, the Dragon Balls clustered together and rose into the air. They flashed a brilliant light, then ZOOM! Each ball rocketed off in a different direction.

"The pig did it!" Yamcha cried.

"Ha ha!" Bulma laughed. "The brat came through!"

"Grampa!" Goku called. While the others cheered, he watched helplessly as Sushinchu, his Grampa's four-star ball, zoomed out of sight.

"Huh? Oh, sorry, kid," Bulma sighed. "But that's what happens after Shen Long grants a wish. All the Dragon Balls scatter who-knows-where. Even your Grampa."

Back outside the castle, Pilaf still couldn't believe what had just happened. "It's not FAIR!" he wailed, searching the sky for any sign of the balls or the dragon. "That was my wish!"

When it was clear that it was all over, really truly over, Pilaf's shock turned to rage. He turned slowly and looked behind him.

Oolong was struggling to pull the underpants over his ears. "They're too small to cover my tail," he explained to Pu'ar. "But maybe I can use them to keep my head war–" The pig looked up. Shu and Mai had them surrounded.

"For stealing my wish," Pilaf snarled, "you will *pay*."

Chapter Two

TANG
TANG

"Some escape!" Yamcha cried. "Now we're in deeper trouble than we were before!" He slammed against the thick steel walls of their new prison. "We won't be smashing through any walls *this* time."

"We did the best we could," Oolong shrugged. "They had huge laser guns! We're lucky to be a—"

"Oh, stop lying," Bulma snapped, eyeing Oolong's head. "And what's with the tighty whities?"

"Well, Miss Swee-Trots," Oolong replied, "as long as you're around, I thought it'd be a good idea to have a spare pair."

Bulma looked at him and snapped the elastic waistband against his forehead before he could say another word.

"Hey, look!" Goku cried, pointing up. "The top of this room's wide open. We can break out of here, no problem!"

"That's a window," Bulma sighed. "And it's probably made of shatterproof glass."

But Goku wasn't listening. He crouched low then sprung straight up toward the ceiling.

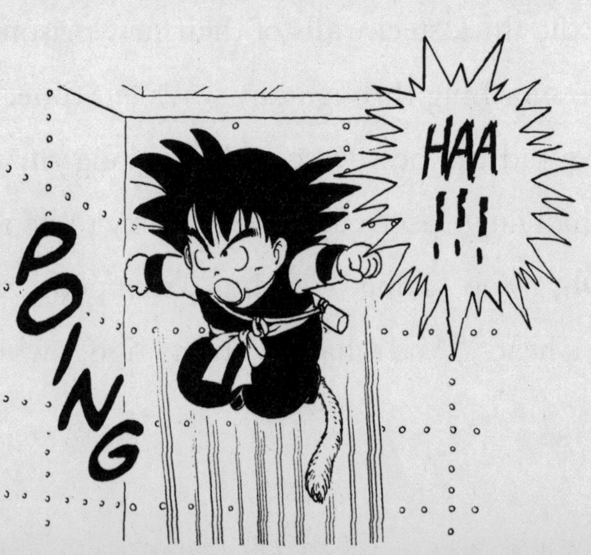
HAA!!!
POING

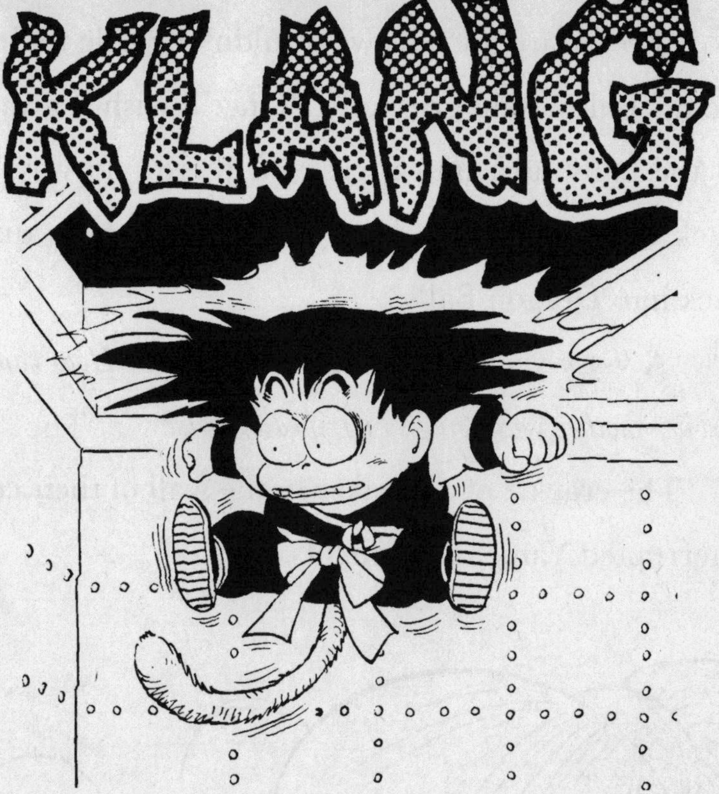
KLANG

KLAANG! He smashed his head against the window and slammed back down to the floor.

"Ow ow ow!" Goku moaned.

"Toldja so," Bulma said.

"Dang it!" Yamcha cried. "If we don't find a way out, we'll die in here. "Then we'll never be able to find those Dragon Balls again!"

"Even if we got out, we wouldn't be able to find them," Bulma said grumpily. "Once a wish is granted the balls turn into rocks and there's no way to track them. It takes at least a year for them to turn back into Dragon Balls."

"A y-y-y-year?" Yamcha stammered. *How can I survive another year being so terrified of girls?*

The crackle of a speaker in the wall of their cell interrupted Yamcha's thoughts.

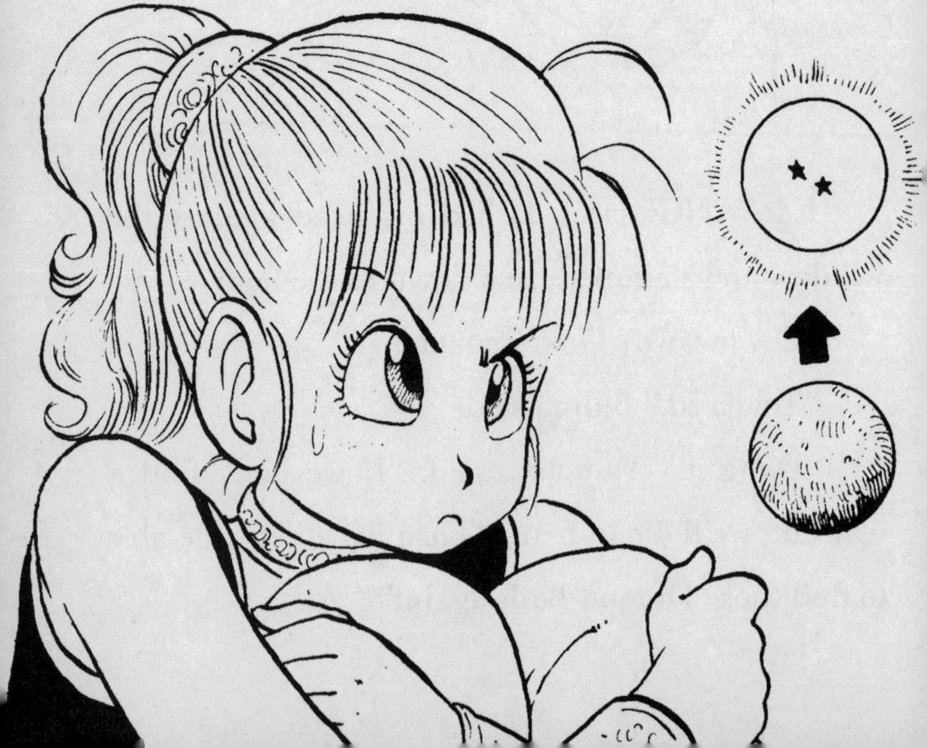

"Prisoners!" the speaker sputtered. "It is I, the great and powerful Pilaf! Like your new digs? I hope so, because this is the last place you'll ever see!

"You may have noticed that the roof of your tomb is made of glass," Pilaf continued. Goku rubbed his head and nodded. "Like a lid on a giant metal pot. Tomorrow, as the sun rises, it will heat your cell, cooking you up slowly like a five-course meal! Bwah ha ha! Sweet dreams!"

"No, no, no!" Bulma wailed. "I'm too cute to be cooked!"

"I don't wanna be a roast!" Oolong squealed.

"I'll never get married!" Yamcha moaned.

"I need to use the little shape-shifter's room!" Pu'ar groaned.

"I'm hungry..." Goku said, holding his stomach.

"Bwah ha ha!" Pilaf cackled. "Sweet dreams!"

"Goku! Yamcha!" Bulma cried. "You've got to get us out of here! I know you're too strong to let a little steel stop you!"

For the next hour, Yamcha and Goku pounded and kicked at the walls and ceiling of their cell with all their might while Bulma cheered them on. Goku even tried the Kamehameha, but nothing worked. Soon they all slumped to the floor, exhausted.

"There's nothing we can do," Yamcha sighed.

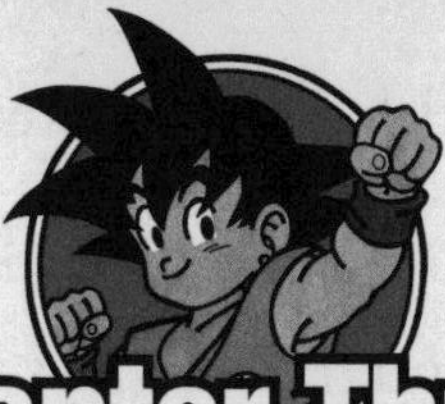

Chapter Three

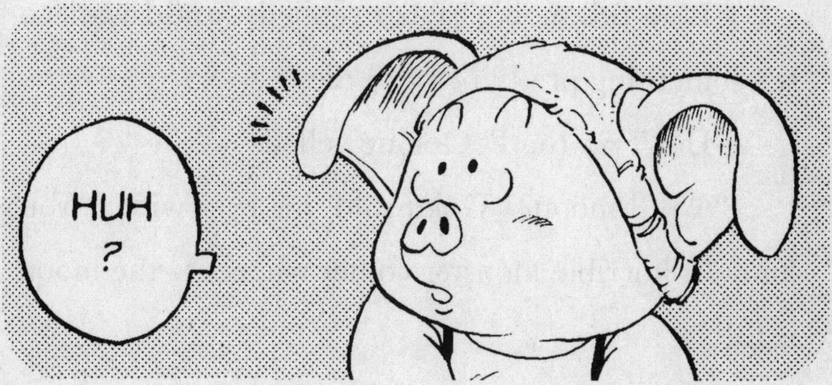
HUH
?

"So this is how it ends, huh?" Oolong sighed.

"No! I won't hear it!" Bulma sobbed. "I do *not* like dying!"

"Who does?" Oolong snapped. "Hey, where's Pu'ar?"

Oolong looked left, he looked right, and finally he looked up. The little cat was floating high in the air, staring out through the glass ceiling. "Pu'ar?"

"I'm looking at the moon," Pu'ar sighed.

"How can you care about the *moon* at a time like this?"

"It's a full moon," Pu'ar replied, "and I want to see something pretty before I die."

"Don't *say* that!" Oolong yelled.

"A full moon?" Goku said, his eyes wide. "You know, a horrible monster comes whenever the moon is full."

"What?" Bulma grumbled. "We're telling camp-fire stories now?"

"It's true!" Goku said. "My grampa died when the monster stepped on him!"

"You're telling us this monster crushed the powerful master Son-Gohan?" Yamcha asked.

"And my house an' trees an' everything!" Goku said.

"Whoa," Oolong breathed. "What did this monster look like?"

"I don't know," Goku said. "I was asleep."

"You *slept* while your house was being smashed?" Oolong said.

Goku thought for a moment. "Grampa always used to say, 'Goku, never look at the full moon, boy...' Weird, huh? I never understood what just lookin' at the moon could do."

Oolong stared at him. He felt the little hairs on the back of his neck rise. A thought was occurring to him, and he didn't like it. He looked at Bulma, then at Yamcha, then Pu'ar. Judging by the looks on their faces, he was sure they were all thinking the same thing. All at once, they zipped to the farthest corner of the cell.

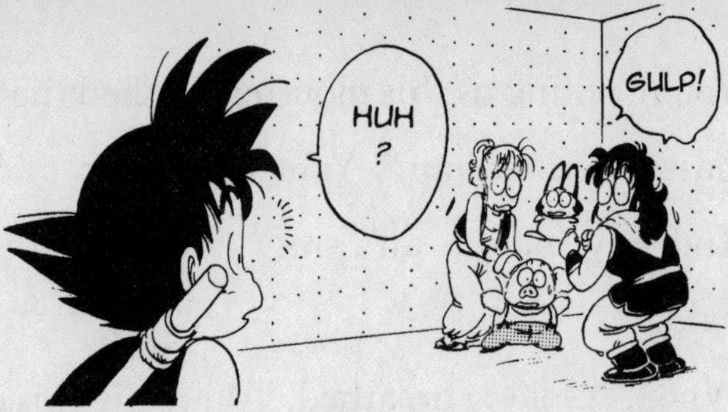
HUH
?
GULP!

"Huh?" Goku said. "What's wrong?"

"T-t-tell m-me s-s-something," Bulma said. "The n-n-night your grampa died...did...did you look at the moon?"

"Yup!" Goku said with an embarrassed laugh. "He told me not to, but I went outside to pee, and... well...heh heh..."

"I *knew* he was no ordinary kid," Yamcha whispered to Bulma.

"It c-c-could be just a c-c-coincidence," Bulma whispered back. "R-right?"

"What is it?" Goku said, still chuckling. "Whatcha talking about?"

"We've got to test it," Oolong said. "Let him see the moon. Then we'll know."

"Yeah," Bulma said. "But if we're right…"

"Wak!" Oolong yelped. "Right! No moon! No moon!"

"You hear that, Goku?" Bulma called. "Whatever you do, don't look up *there*!"

She pointed.

"Up *there*?" Goku asked, following Bulma's hand. And there was the full moon.

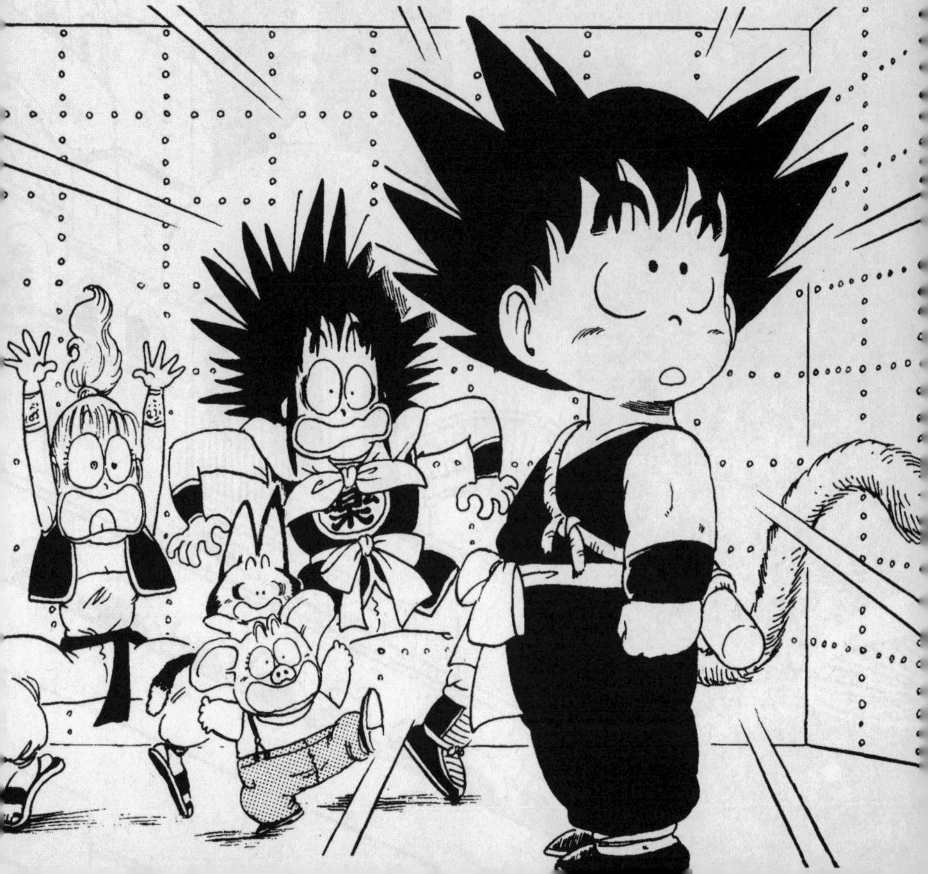

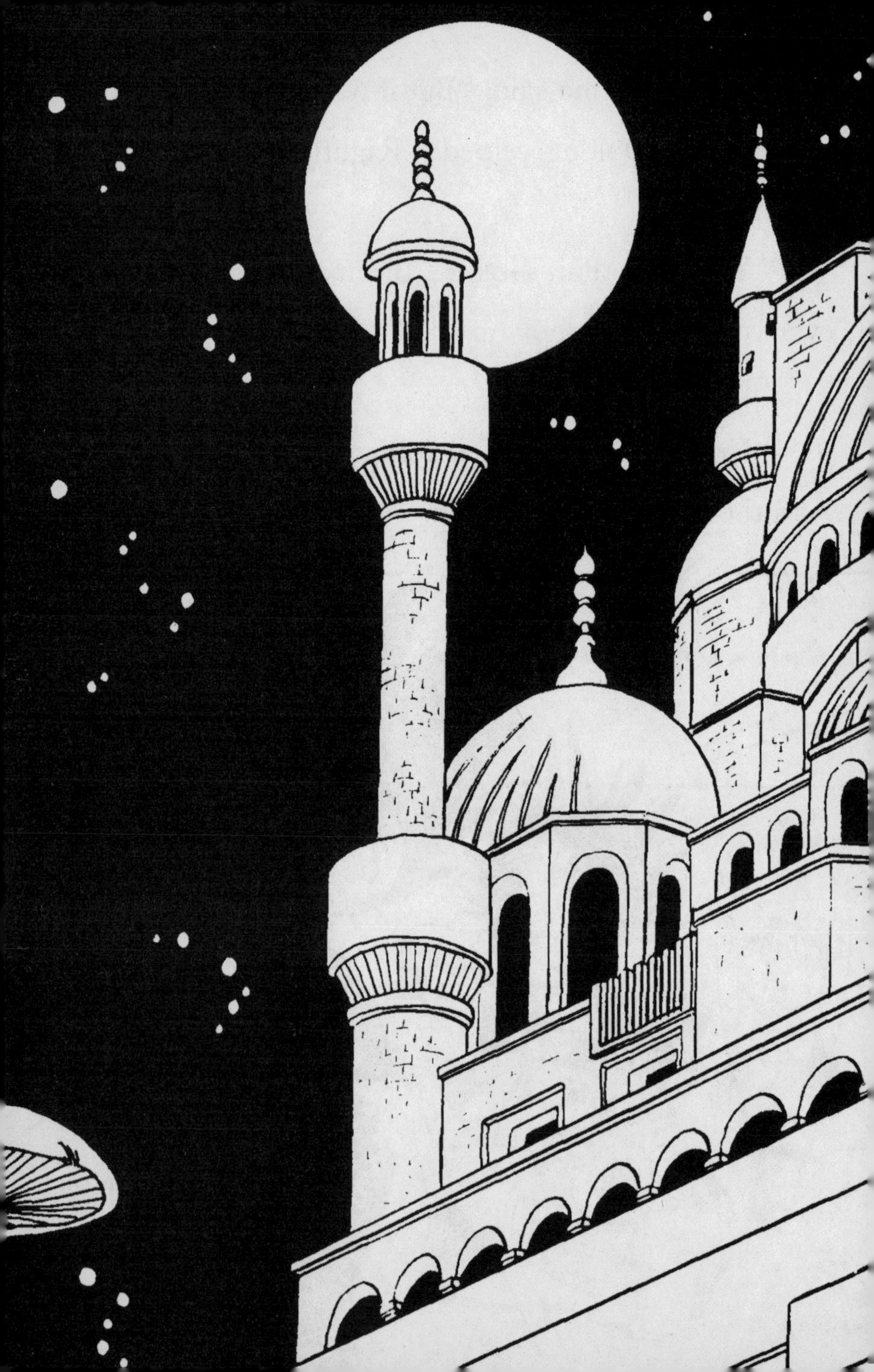

Goku froze. His eyes locked on the moon and grew to the size of small saucers. Bulma, Yamcha, Oolong, and Pu'ar watched, too afraid to move.

Then Goku laughed. "Oops," he said, turning toward them. "I did it again!"

"Y-y-you're okay?" Oolong breathed. "N-n-nothing's...wrong?"

"What could be wrong?" Goku asked.

"Phew!" Yamcha sighed.

"Phew!" Pu'ar sighed.

"Don't scare us like that!" Oolong laughed.

"I told you it was just a coincidence!" Bulma snapped, wiping the sweat from her brow.

But Goku didn't answer. He had suddenly gone stiff as a board.

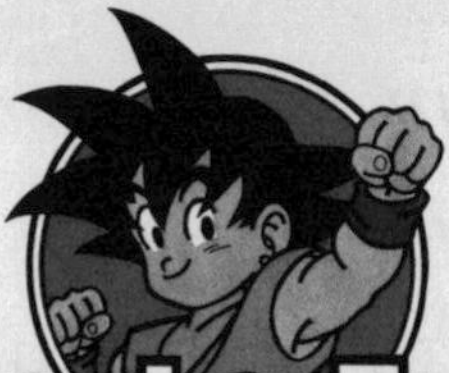

Chapter Four

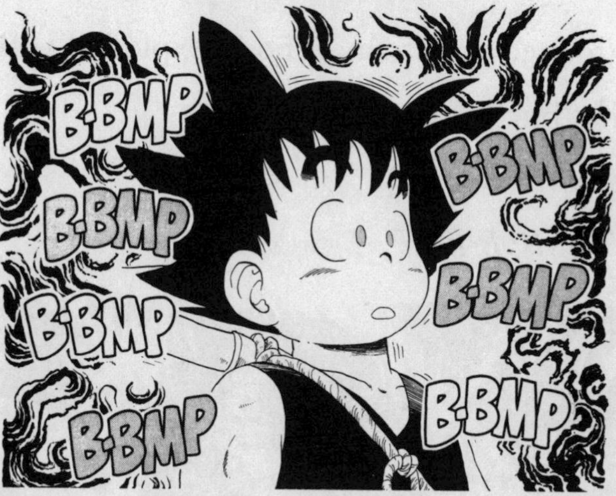
B-BMP
B-BMP
B-BMP
B-BMP
B-BMP
B-BMP
B-BMP

B-BMP B-BMP

Goku's eyes glazed over and he began to tremble.

B-BMP B-BMP

"H-hey, buddy. What's wrong?" Oolong stammered.

"S-st-stop joking around," Bulma tried to laugh, but it's hard to laugh when you can hardly breathe.

B-BMP B-BMP

B-BMP B-BMP

Suddenly, Goku's crazy shock of hair blew straight up. His eyes rolled back. He gritted his teeth and groaned as his small body exploded with muscles that burst through his clothes.

B-BMP B-BMP

B-BMP B-BMP

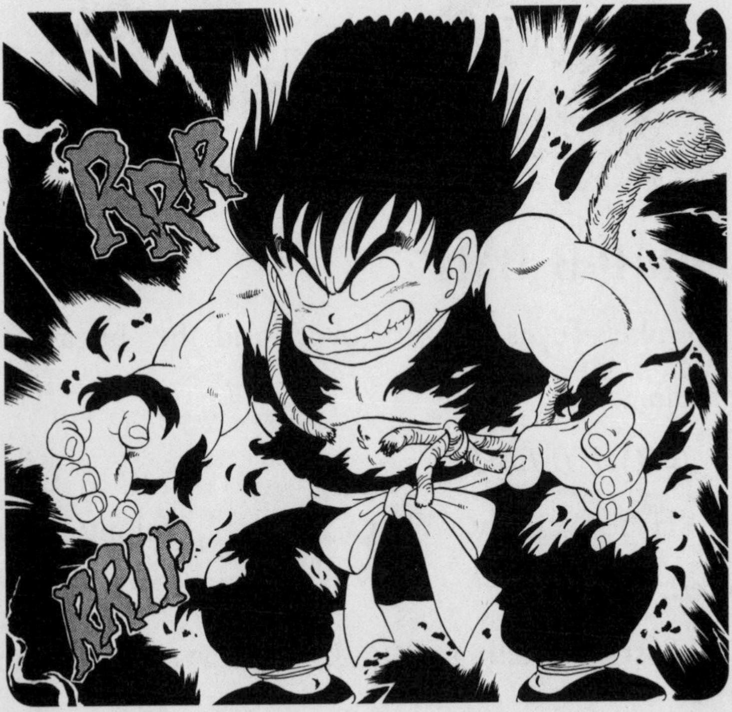
RRR
RRIP

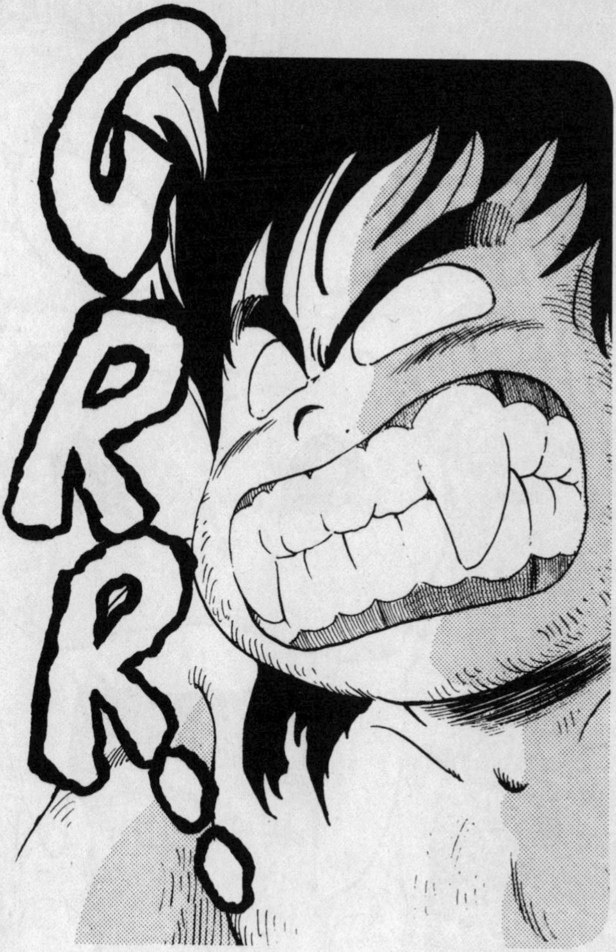
GRRR...

Goku's teeth lengthened and curved into sharp fangs. He strained as his jaw expanded and stretched into a powerful muzzle. Thick dark hair sprouted from his face, his back, his arms–everywhere. And through it all, Goku grew.

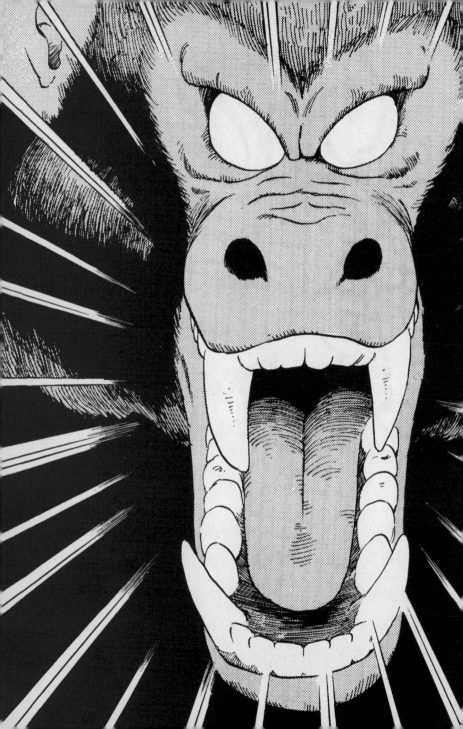

He grew and grew until he was nearly ten times his normal size–too massive to be contained by Pilaf's puny prison. Finally, with a mighty RAAWR! he shattered the shatterproof ceiling.

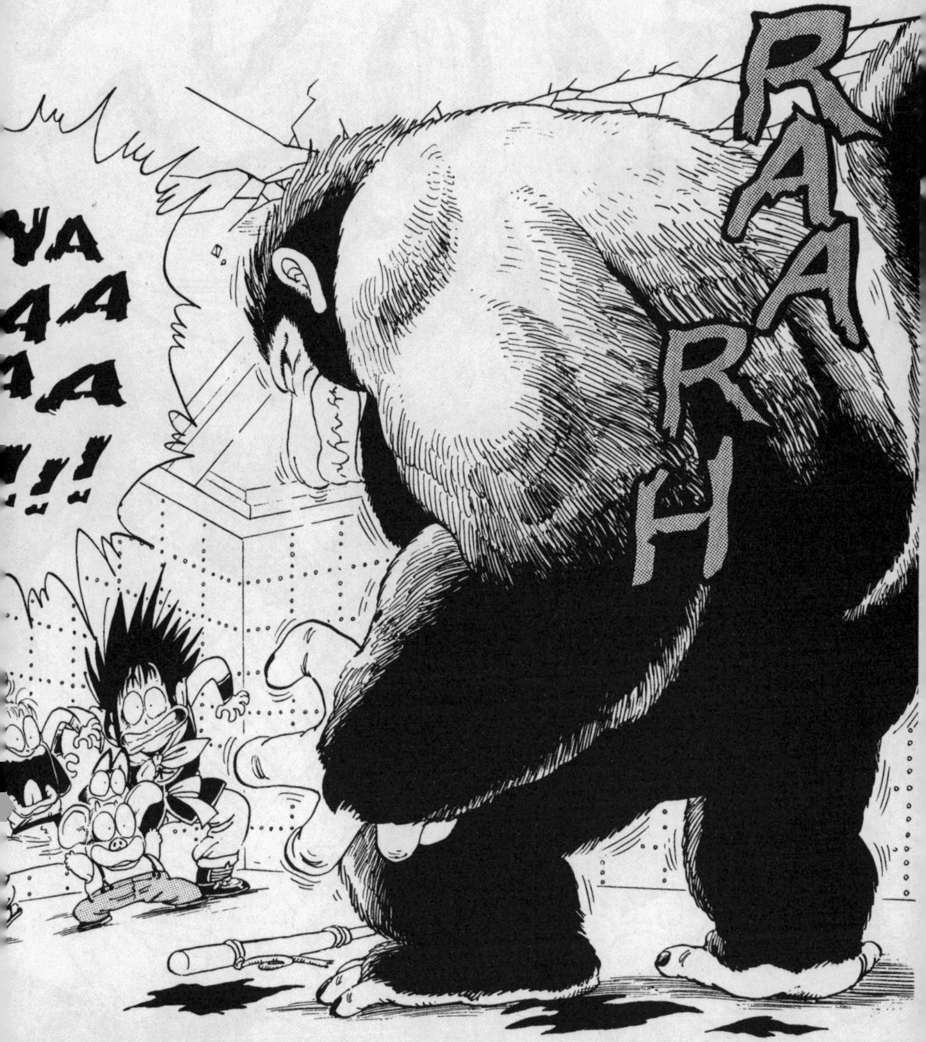
RAARH

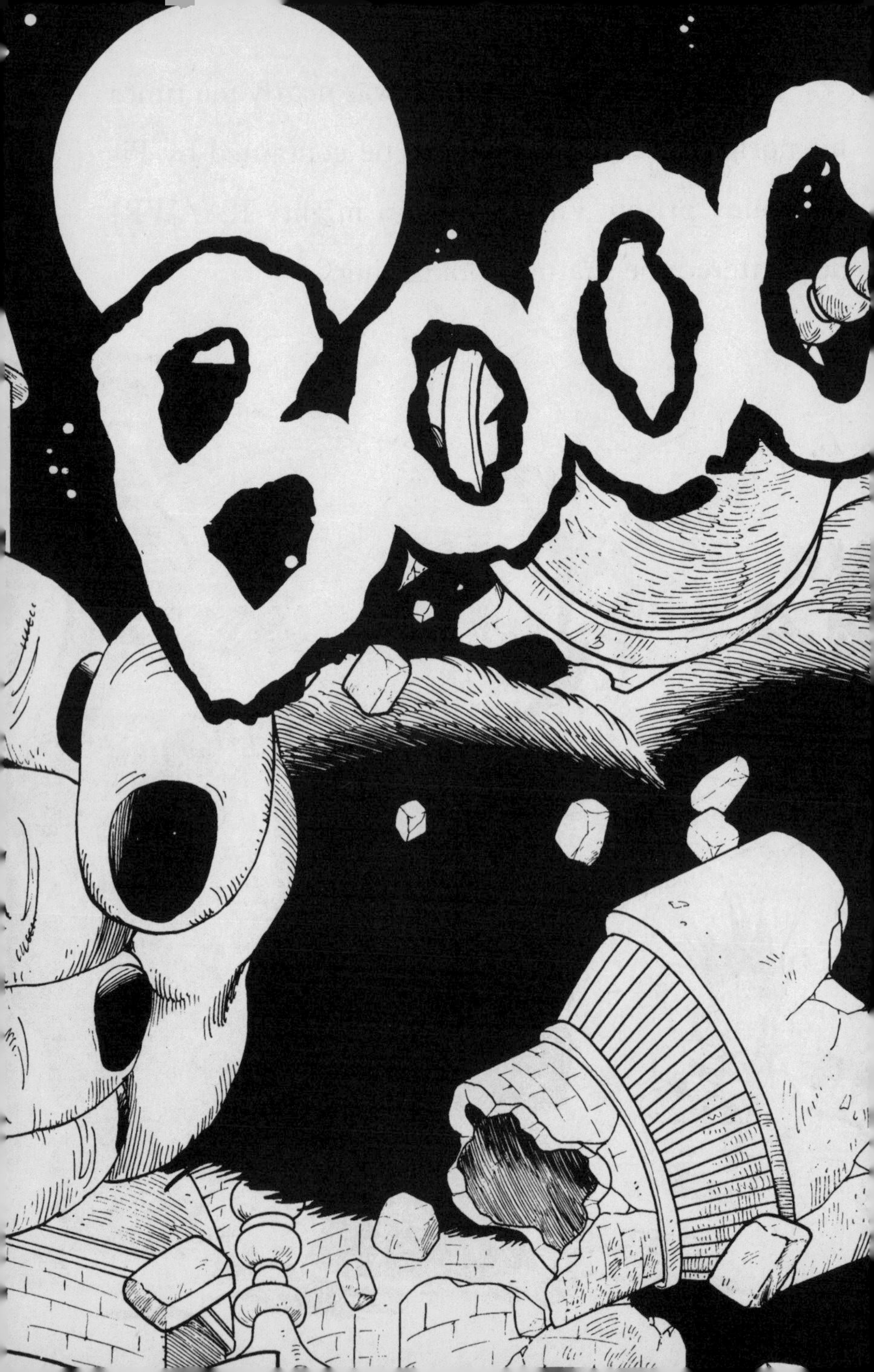
BOOO

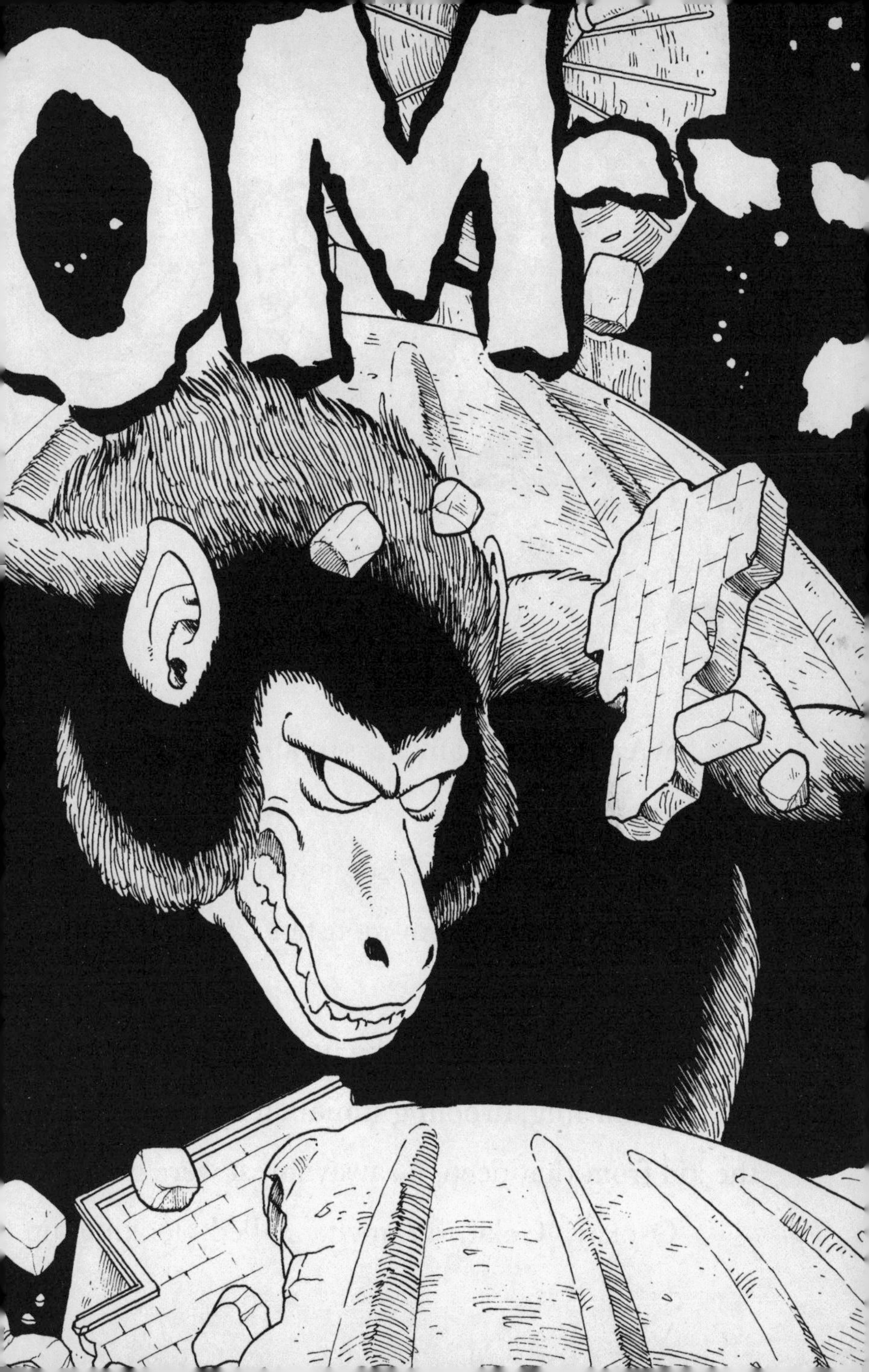
OM

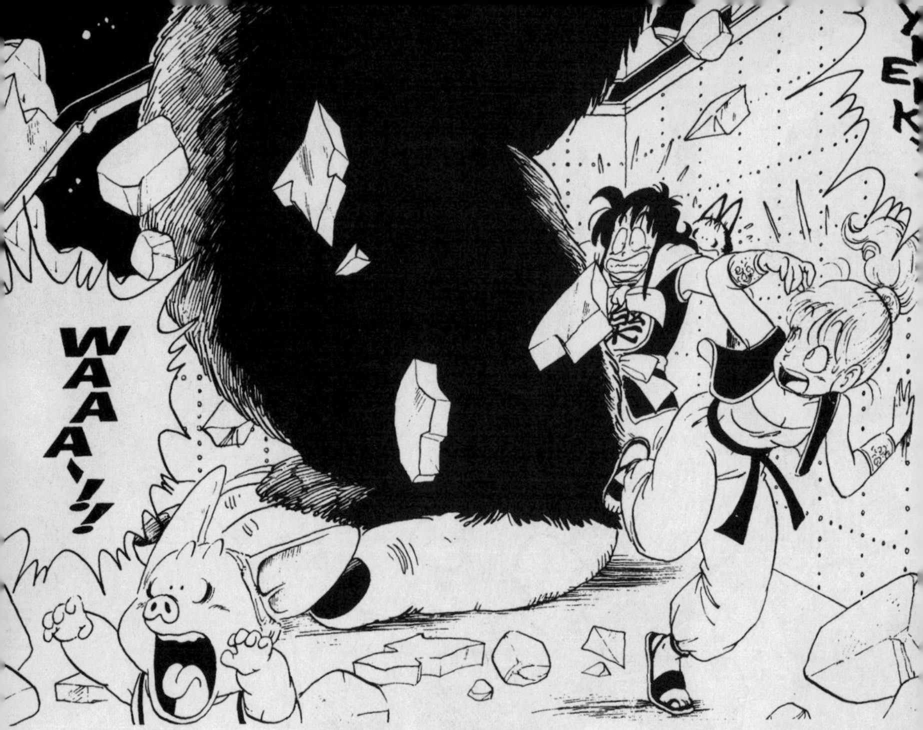
YEEK
WAAAA!!

"WAAAAA!" Yamcha screamed, dodging the falling debris.

"He's a *m-m-monster*!" screamed Pu'ar.

"A *m-m-monkey* m-m-monster!" screamed Bulma.

And she was right. Goku had transformed into a colossal snarling, drooling simian beast. All traces of the kid from that deep, faraway forest were gone.

"O-okay, Goku." Yamcha called, looking up

at the beast. "You-you can change back now. You smashed the r-roof. We're free!"

But Goku wasn't listening.

At the sound of the shattered glass, Emperor Pilaf woke up.

"Huh?" he yawned. "Whazzat?"

"Sounds like the prisoners are getting rowdy," Mai said, rubbing her eyes.

"The nerve of them disturbing our—"

KABOOM! Goku smashed through Pilaf's tower bedroom.

"WHAT'S HAPPENING?!" Pilaf cried, just before Goku's gigantic fist slammed down on his bed.

AIEE!!

WHAT'S HAPPENING?!

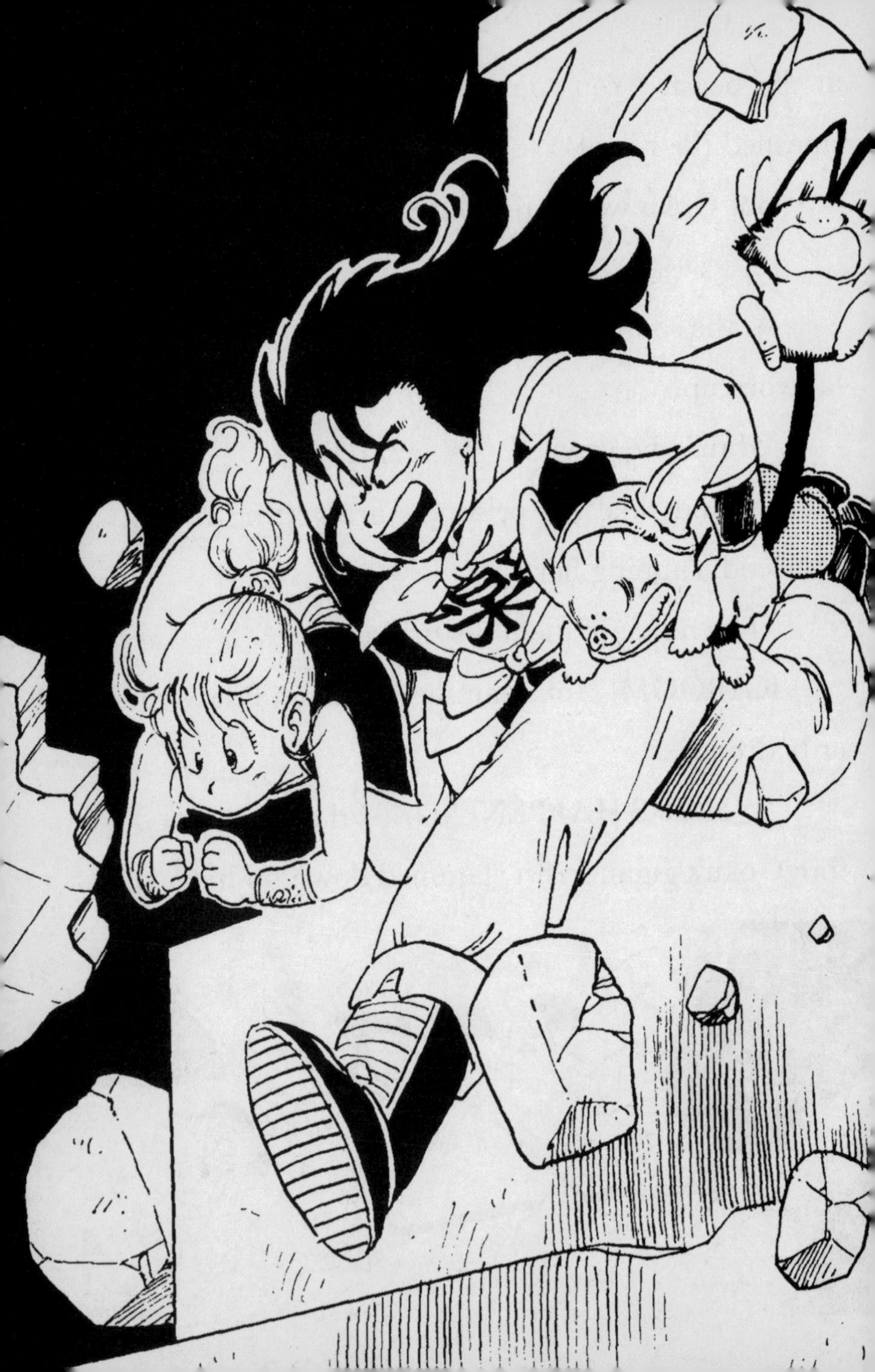
楽

"WAAAAA!" The tiny tyrant ran from the ruins of his bedroom to the hangar where he kept his plane.

"START THE ENGINES! START THE ENGINES!" he cried to Shu and Mai, who were already there.

Meanwhile, Yamcha had grabbed Bulma in one arm and Oolong and Pu'ar in the other and was hightailing it from ruins of the castle. Behind them, Goku—who was now taller than the castle and nearly twice as wide—was smashing the palace to bits. All around them, stone walls came crashing down.

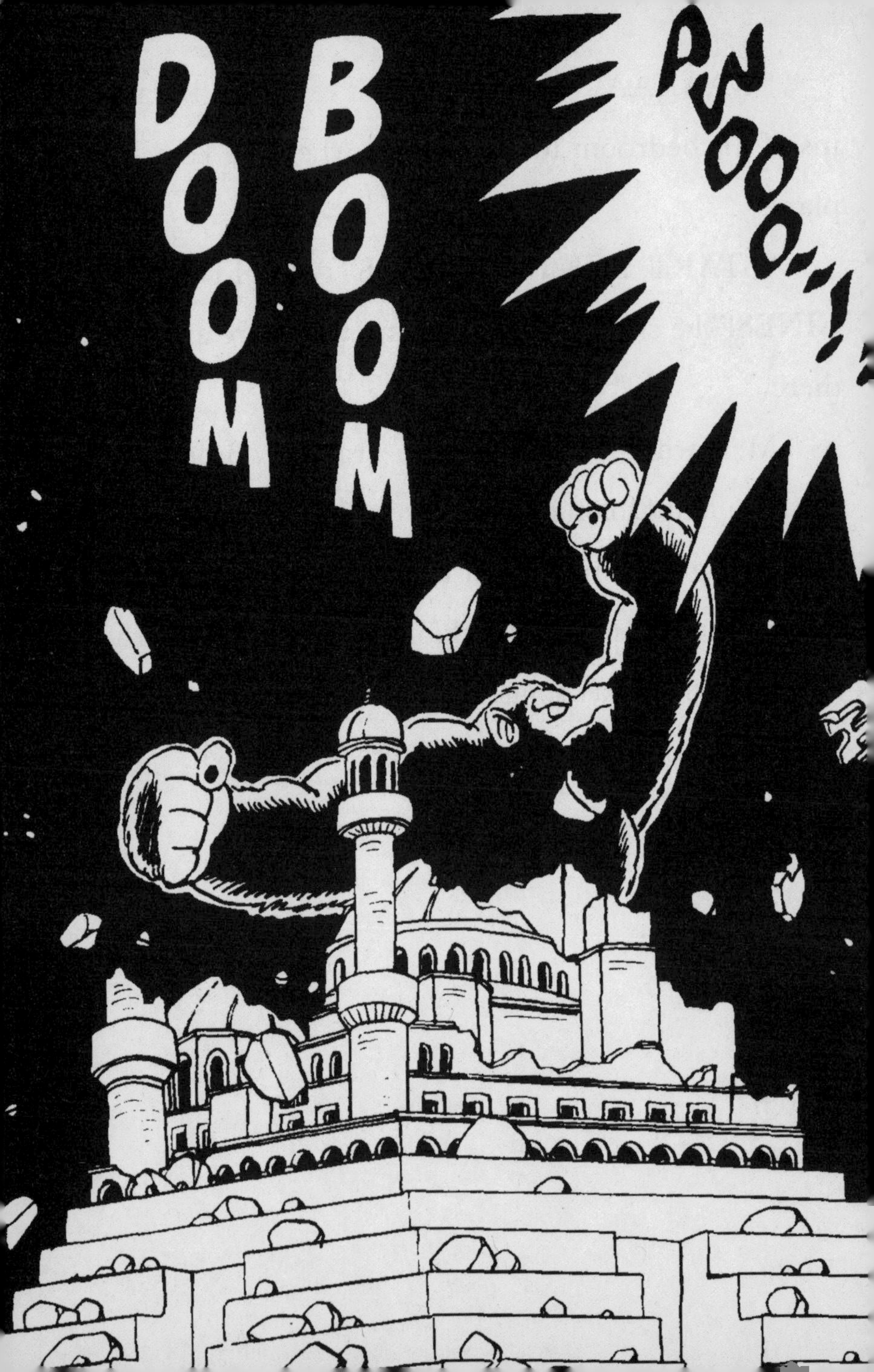
PWOOO--!!
BOOOM
DOOOM

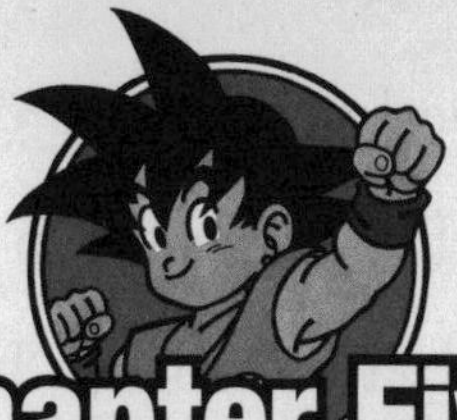

Chapter Five

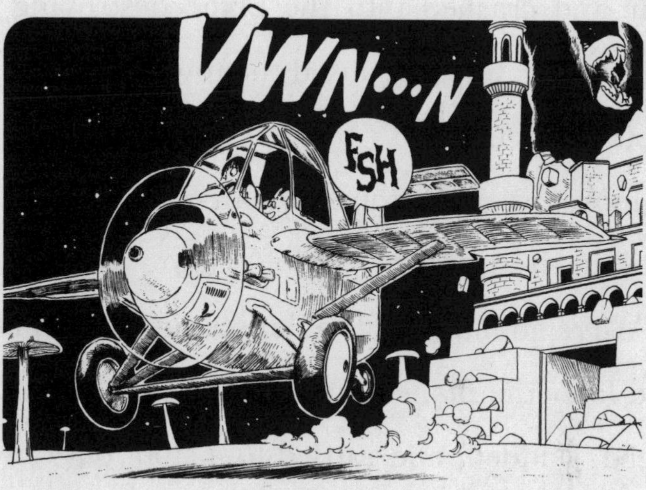
VWN...N
FSH

On the other side of the wreckage, Mai had started the plane.

"Take off!! Take off!!!" Pilaf cried.

The plane sputtered and started to lift.

"We made it!" Mai cried. "We're safe! Wah-hoo!"

As Goku ripped off the top of the castle's tallest tower, he spotted the aircraft. He lifted the stone turret above his head and with all his might, heaved it at the disappearing plane.

Like a giant missile of stone it whistled through the air and crashed into the plane destroying the back end. The impact caused the tower to rocket off in another direction.

Smoke billowed from the half of the plane that was still in the air.

"We're gonna crash!" Pilaf screamed, and not a second later the plane plummeted to the ground. It bounced, skidded, and rattled to a stop, but not before its passengers were hurled into the sand. Slowly, Shu, Mai, and Pilaf raised their heads.

"Who was that?" Pilaf groaned.

Meanwhile, Yamcha and the others ran faster than any of them had ever run in their lives. They raced around a pile of fallen stones...and before them lay nothing but the open desert. They had left the

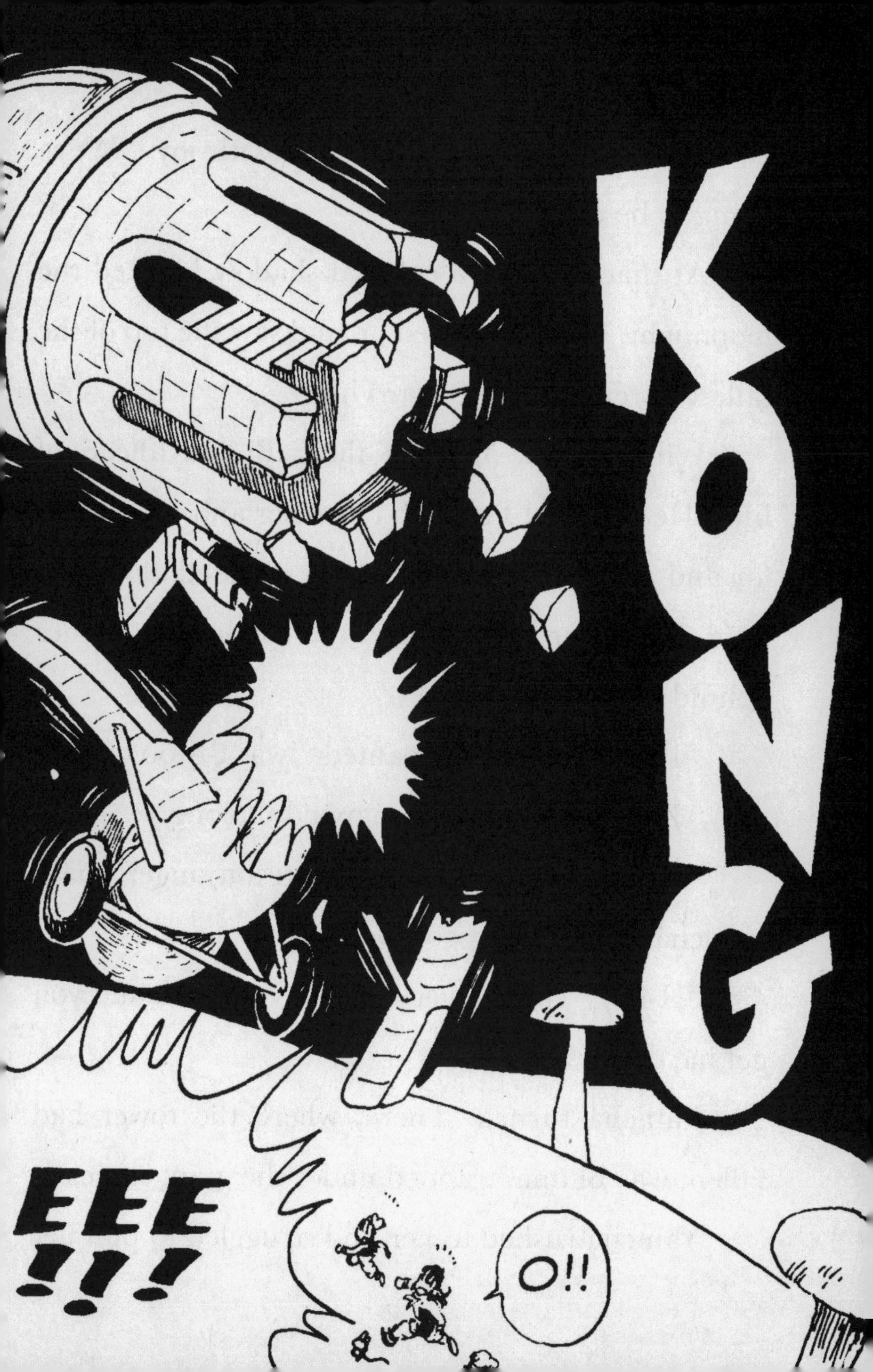
KONG
O!!
EEE!!!

rubble of the palace behind!

"We made it!" Yamcha cried with joy. "We're going to be okay!"

At that moment a colossal shadow blocked the moonlight. Yamcha looked up and saw the top of the tallest tower hurtling toward him.

With a roar, Yamcha flung Bulma ahead of him. He grabbed Pu'ar and Oolong and jumped as far and as fast as he could. As he skidded along the sand, the tower crashed into the earth mere inches behind him.

"Th-th-that," Pu'ar panted, "was t-t-too close."

"That stupid Goku!" snapped Oolong.

"We don't have time to waste on anger now," Yamcha said. "We've got to…"

"H-hey," came a very scared voice. "Could you get me out of here?"

Yamcha turned. There, where the tower had fallen, was Bulma, trapped under the giant stones.

Yamcha rushed to her and struggled to pull her

free. But it was no use. "It's so…heavy!" he grunted. "It won't…budge!"

"Try harder!" Bulma wailed. "Please!"

Yamcha pushed against the tower with all his might. A stone shook loose. Then another. "I think… I'm getting it," he gasped.

"I hate to tell you this," Oolong said. "But I don't think you did that."

BOOM. BOOM. BOOM. The ground shook. Then:

ROOAR!

"He's coming!" Oolong cried. "GOKU'S COMING!"

Step by enormous step the monkey-monster drew closer. And closer. And closer.

"We're gonna be smashed!" Oolong cried.

"Not today, we're not," Bulma snapped. "Goku! Stop this right now!" she cried. "This isn't funny anymore!"

Goku lifted his massive foot.

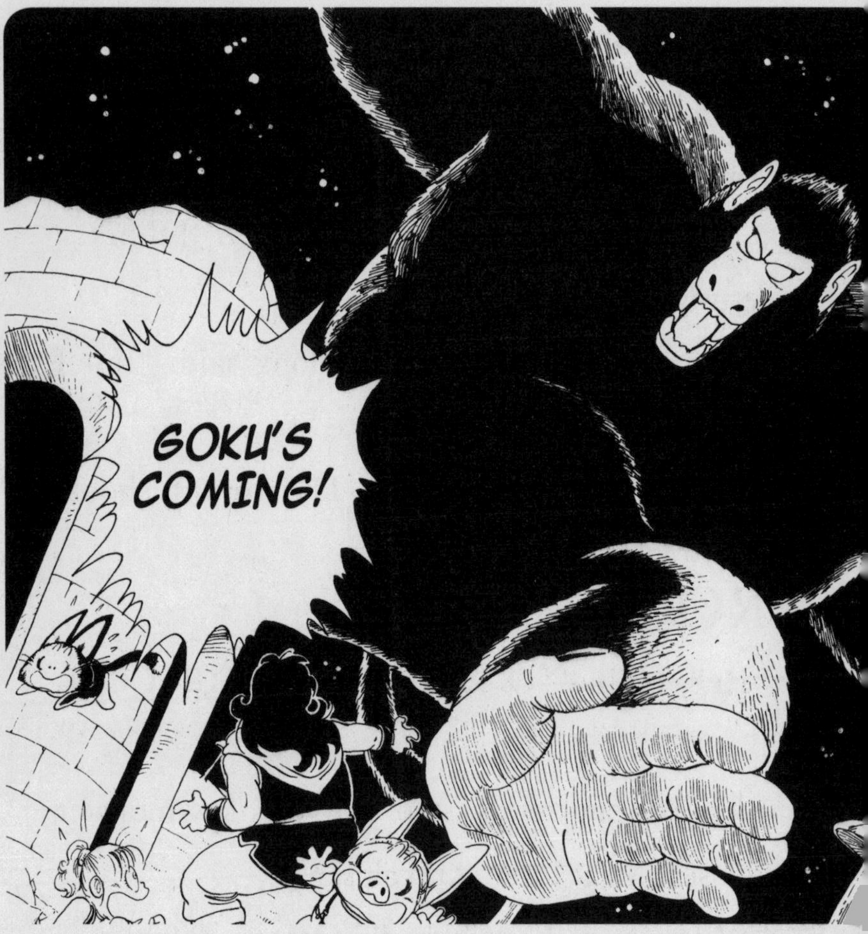
GOKU'S COMING!

"What do I do?" Yamcha asked. "I can't leave leave Bulma! But..."

"Lord Yamcha!" cried Pu'ar. "His weakness!"

"Weakness?" Yamcha asked.

“Remember? When we were spying on him in the desert? And that girl accidentally grabbed him by–”

“His tail!” Yamcha gasped. “But is it still his weakness when he’s a monster?”

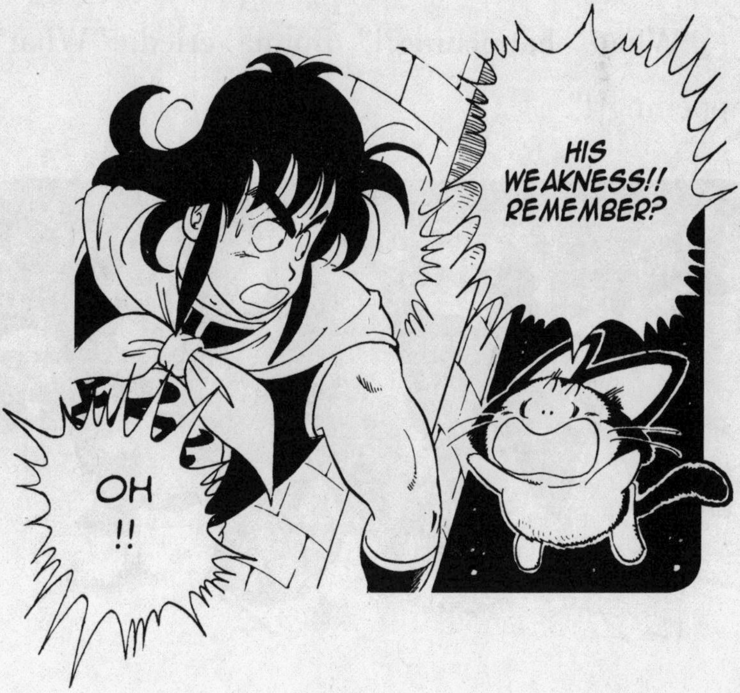
HIS WEAKNESS!! REMEMBER?
OH !!

Goku was bringing his titanic foot back down. In seconds, the stone tower would be crushed, and Bulma with it.

"Only one way to find out!"

Yamcha raced under Goku's foot and wrapped his arms around the monkey-monster's tail. He squeezed with all his strength.

Goku froze. He trembled a bit and took a step backward.

"What's happening?!" Bulma cried. "What's happening?!"

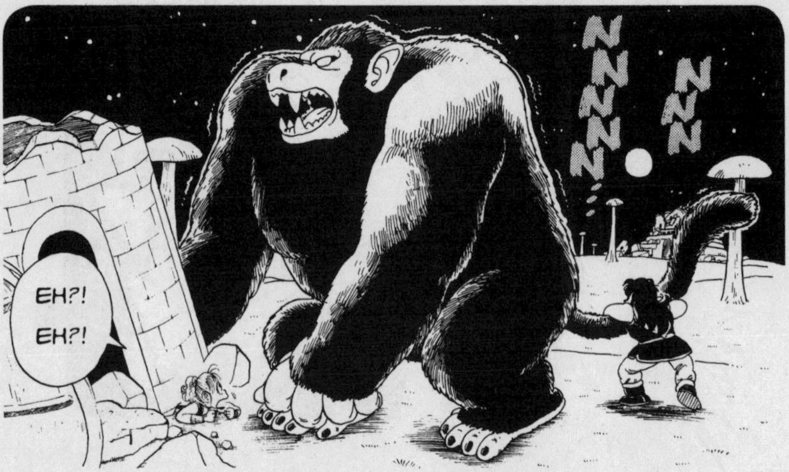
NNNNN
NNN
EH?! EH?!

"Yes!" Pu'ar crowed. "It's working!"

"I can't hold him forever!" Yamcha cried. "Quick! Turn into a pair of giant scissors!"

"Aye, aye, sir!" And–POOF!–Pu'ar was a pair of scissors. With one quick move he snipped off Goku's tail.

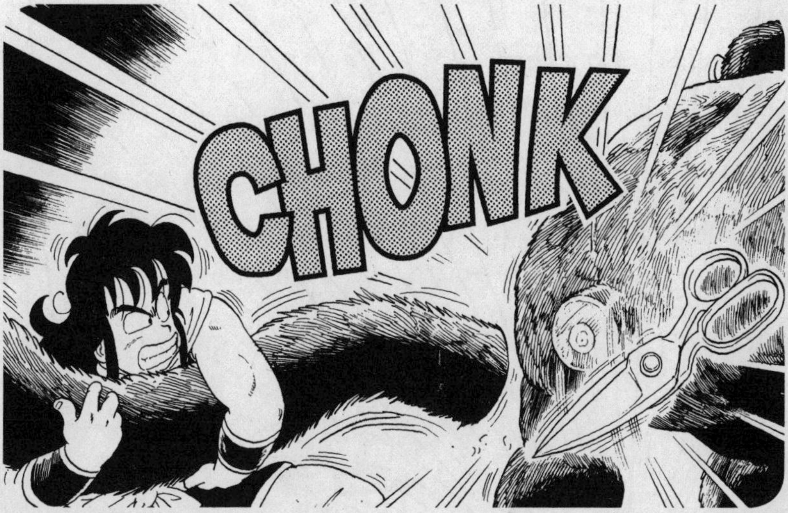
CHONK

Instantly, Goku shrank back to his normal size. His snout withdrew, his teeth shrank, and his fur disappeared. Goku was Goku once again. Without a word, he lay down on the ground and fell fast asleep.

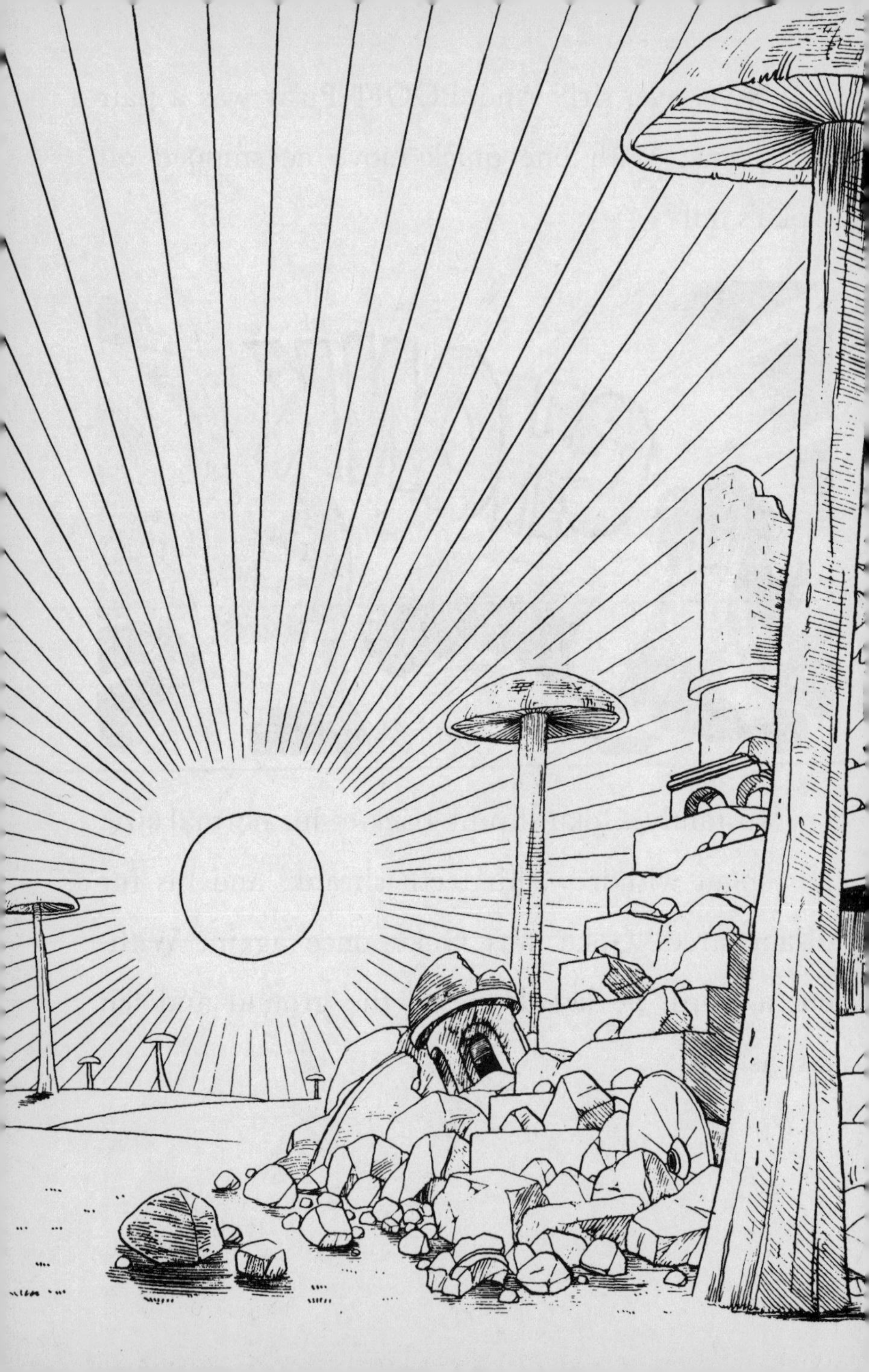

Chapter Six

YAWN...

The next morning the sun rose revealing
a vast pile of stones where once Pilaf's palace had
stood. Of Emperor Pilaf himself and his two lieuten-
ants there was no sign; the wreckage of their plane
lay empty in the sand. Apparently the deadly trio
had snuck off under cover of darkness. There was no
one around except Yamcha, Bulma, Oolong, Pu'ar,
and Goku...who still fast asleep.

"Sheesh," Oolong said, eyeing the boy. "I can't believe what that kid put us through!"

"Oh, cut him some slack," Yamcha said. "He got us out of prison, didn't he?"

"What do you think he is?" Pu'ar wondered. "I've never seen anything like him on earth."

"Whatever he is," said Yamcha, still holding Goku's tail, "without this, he'll never be dangerous like that again."

"Thank goodness," Bulma sighed.

Goku woke with a mighty yawn. "G'morning!" he said with a smile.

"'Good morning'?" Oolong snorted. "Is that all you have to say for yourself?"

"What do you mean?" Goku said. "And—hey! Where're my clothes?"

"You mean...you don't remember *anything*?" Yamcha asked.

"'Bout what?" Goku asked.

"Hold on," Oolong said "You're telling me you

don't remember turning into a—"

Bulma jabbed Oolong hard with her elbow. "No!" she whispered. "We can't tell him. He'll feel awful if he learns that he was the monster who killed his own grandfather!"

"What about how awful *I* feel for almost getting squished by him too?" Oolong shot back. But Bulma gave him such an angry look that he didn't say another word.

"What're you guys whispering about?" Goku asked, getting to his feet.

"Getting you some clothes," Bulma replied. "Oolong, give him your underpants."

"These came straight from the dragon god himself," Oolong cried, grabbing his head. "No way! I'll give him my pants instead."

"Man, you've got short legs," Goku said, pulling on Oolong's pants. And just as he adjusted the straps on the suspenders—FOOMP!—Goku fell over.

"What was that?" Oolong asked.

"Lost my balance for some reason," Goku replied.

"I hate to have to tell you this," Yamcha said gently, "but I'm afraid it's because...you've lost your *tail*."

"MY TAIL?!" Goku yelled, reaching around to grab his backside. "Whoa! It's gone!"

His friends waited for him to cry or fly into a rage or at least demand to know what had happened. But instead, he just shrugged.

"Oh well," he said.

Oolong slapped his forehead. "I can't believe you! Doesn't anything upset you?"

"Not a little thing like a tail," Goku said. "But where's my nyoi-bo? I'd hate to lose that!"

"It must be buried in that rubble somewhere," Yamcha said.

Goku took off in the direction Yamcha pointed. Then—WOMP—he fell flat on his face. He got up and started running again, and—WOMP—he fell again.

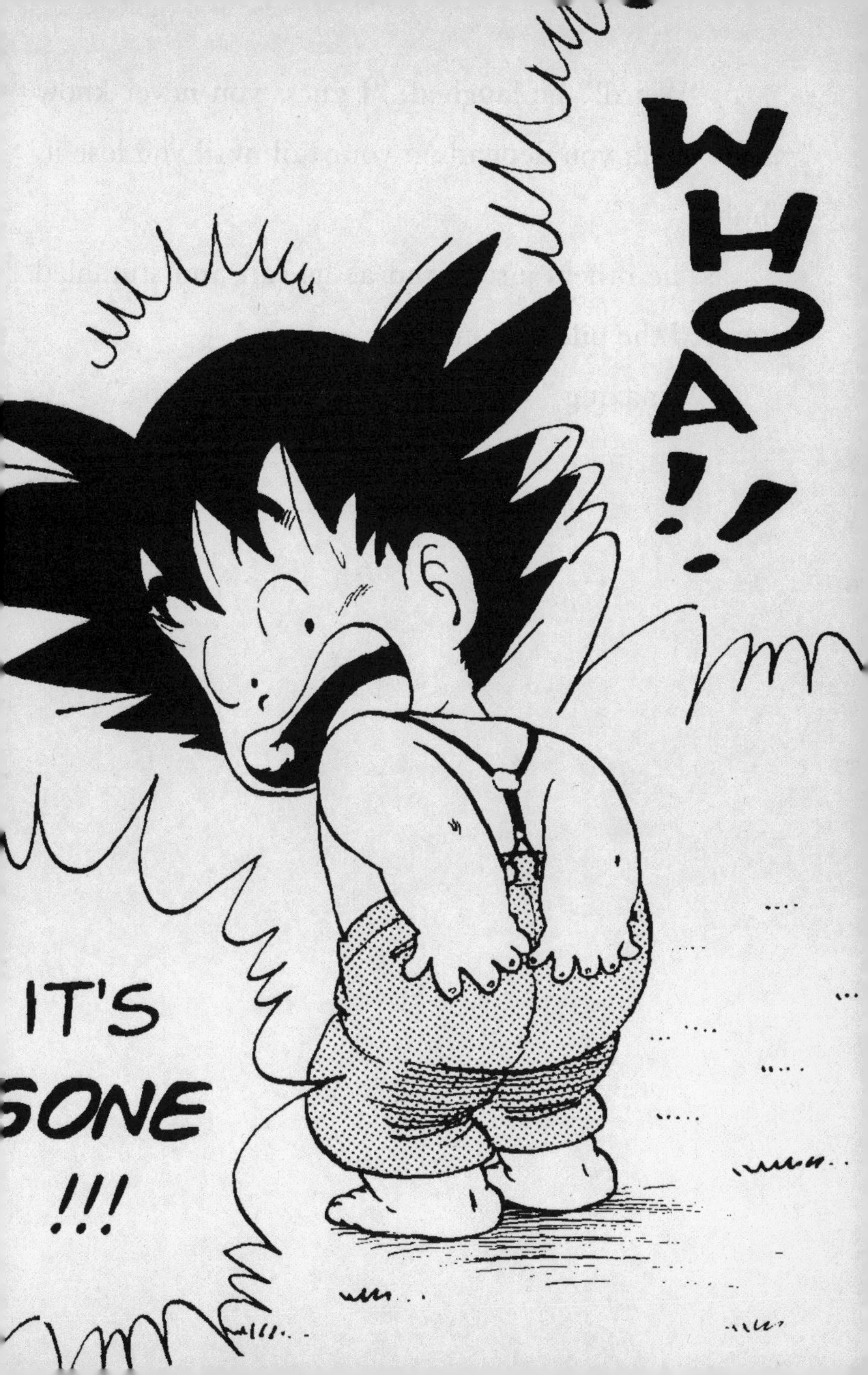
WHOA!!
IT'S GONE !!!

"Weird!" he laughed. "I guess you never know how much you depend on your tail until you lose it, huh?"

The others just stared as he ran and stumbled toward the pile of stone.

"Amazing," Oolong said. "Just...amazing."

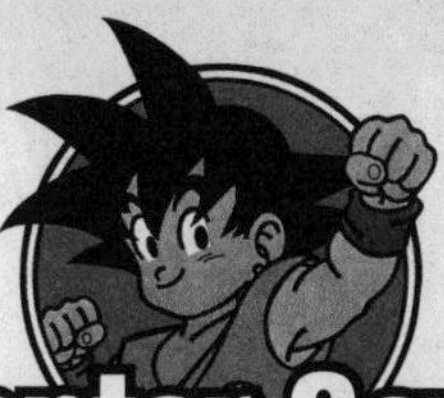

Chapter Seven

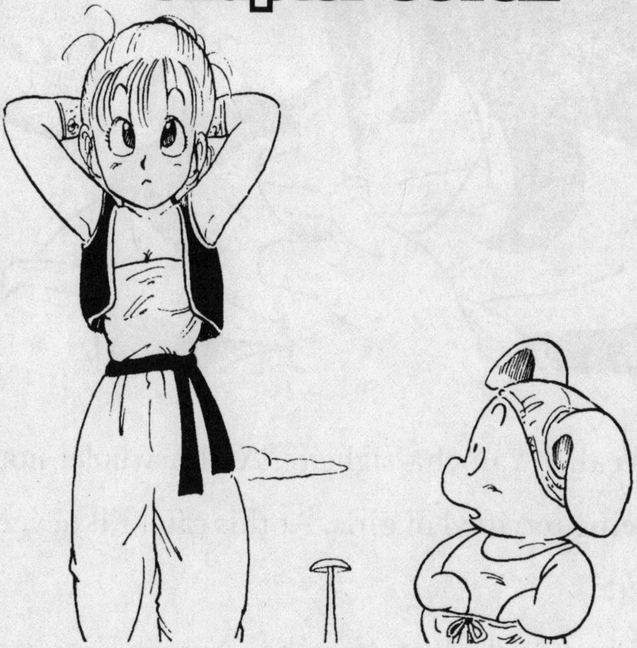

"So what're we gonna do now?" Oolong asked Bulma. "If it'll be a year before we can track the Dragon Balls, we might as well go our separate ways, right?"

"I guess so," Bulma sighed. "That means a whole 'nother year without the perfect boyfriend."

"Yeah," Yamcha sighed. "And a whole 'nother year being terrified of girls. At this rate, I'll never get married."

Bulma looked at Yamcha. Yamcha looked at Bulma.

DING!

"W-w-wait a minute," Yamcha stammered. "*You're* a girl, and well, *sometimes* you can be scary–"

"Hey!" Bulma cried.

"–but I'm not afraid of you!"

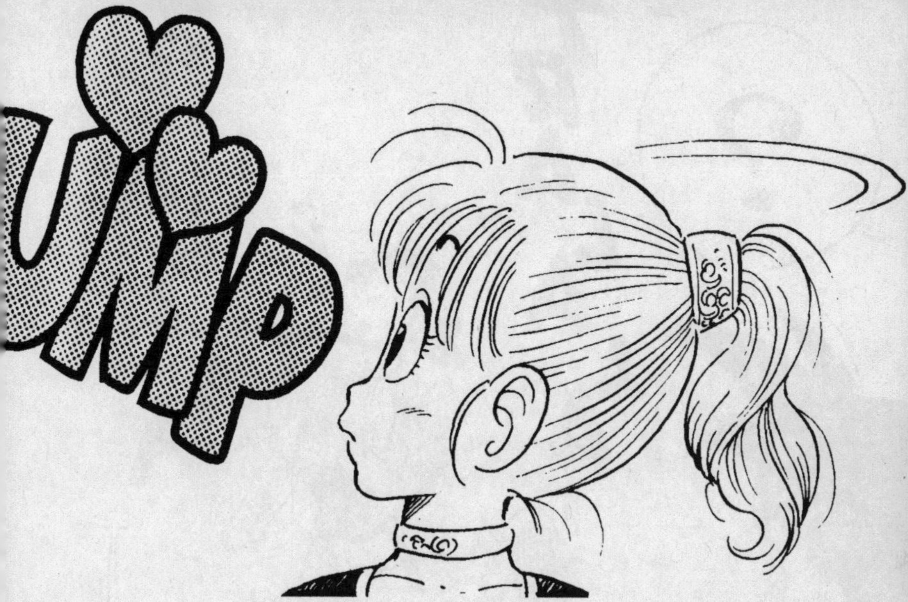
UMP

"And-and you're super cute." Bulma beamed. "Plus, you tried to save me last night! *So romantic*!"

"Then..." Yamcha breathed.

"Maybe we could…?" Bulma breathed.

"Would you like to be my...my…"

"I found it!" Goku cried. He came running back from the rubble with his staff in his hand. Then–WOMP—he fell flat on his face again.

"Look, Oolong!" Goku called again. But Oolong was watching Bulma and Yamcha.

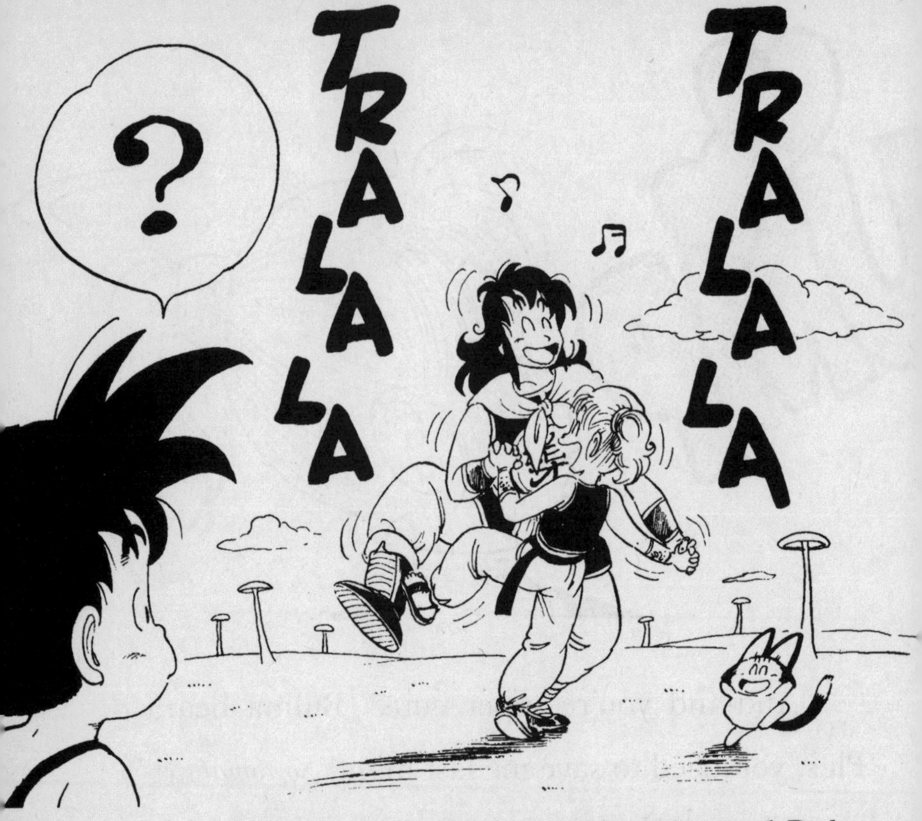
?
TRALALA
TRALALA

Goku looked over and saw Yamcha and Bulma holding hands as they spun in a circle. They hummed and giggled and blushed, and Oolong didn't look too happy about any of it.

"What's going on?" Goku asked.

"They're getting what they've always wanted!" Pu'ar smiled.

"They're making me sick," snorted the pig.

"Goku! Goku!" cried Bulma breathlessly. "Yamcha and I are going back to the city! Together! Do you want to come?"

"Nah. I'm gonna go train with Roshi, the Turtle Guy," Goku replied. "I wanna get really strong!"

"How 'bout you, Oolong? Wanna come?"

"Are there really lots of girls in the city, like everyone says?" Oolong asked.

"Tons and tons!" Bulma said.

"All right!" Oolong said.

"Too bad they won't be into a bore of a boar like you!" Bulma teased.

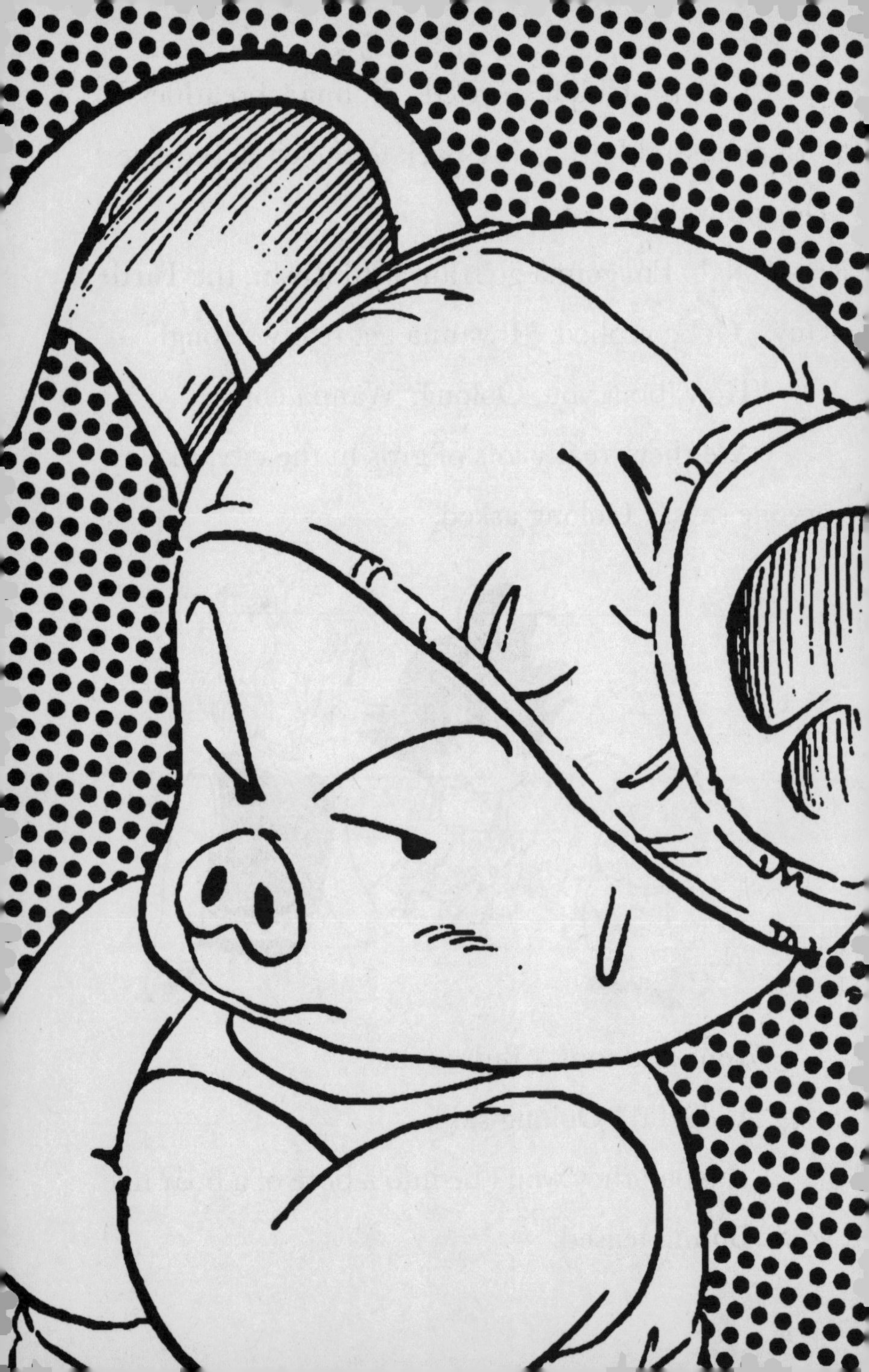

"You could've stopped at 'tons and tons'!" snapped Oolong. "Aw, heck. It's not like I have many options. I guess I'll tag along."

"And next year," Goku grinned, "let's hunt Dragon Balls again, 'kay?"

"Who needs Dragon Balls?" Bulma blushed, looking at Yamcha.

"Not me!" Yamcha blushed, looking at Bulma.

"BLECCH!" gagged Oolong.

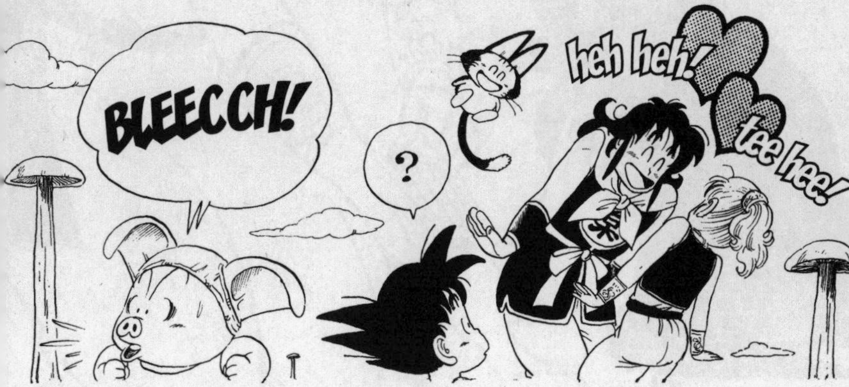
heh heh!
tee hee!
?
BLEECCH!

"But...wait," Goku said. "I've got to get my grampa's ball back! If you're not coming with me, how am I gonna track it?"

"Here," Bulma said. "Take my Dragon Radar!"

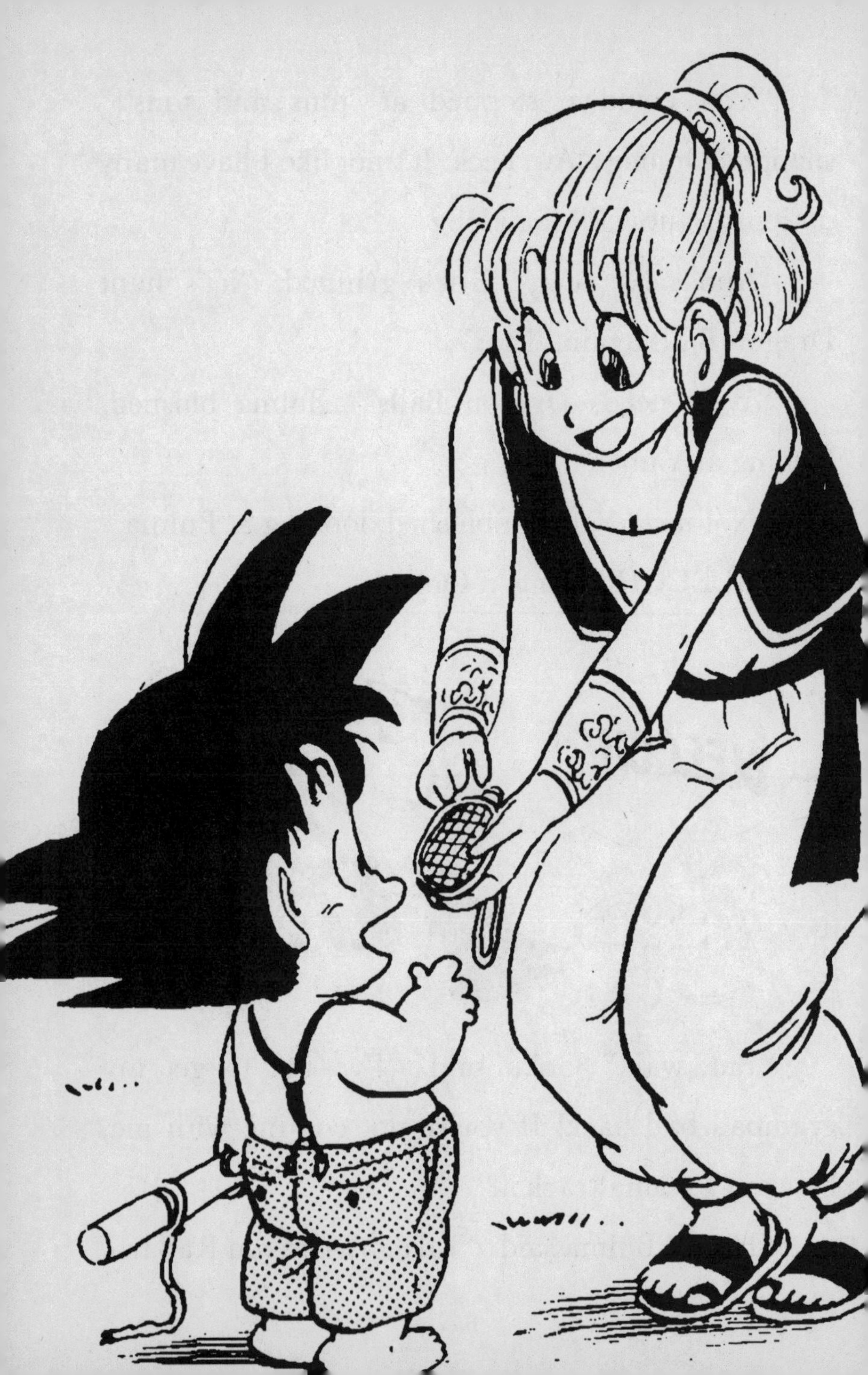

She handed it to Goku and pointed to a big button. "A year from now, press this button. You should get a signal leading you to the closest Dragon Ball."

"Really?" Goku said. "I can hardly wait!"

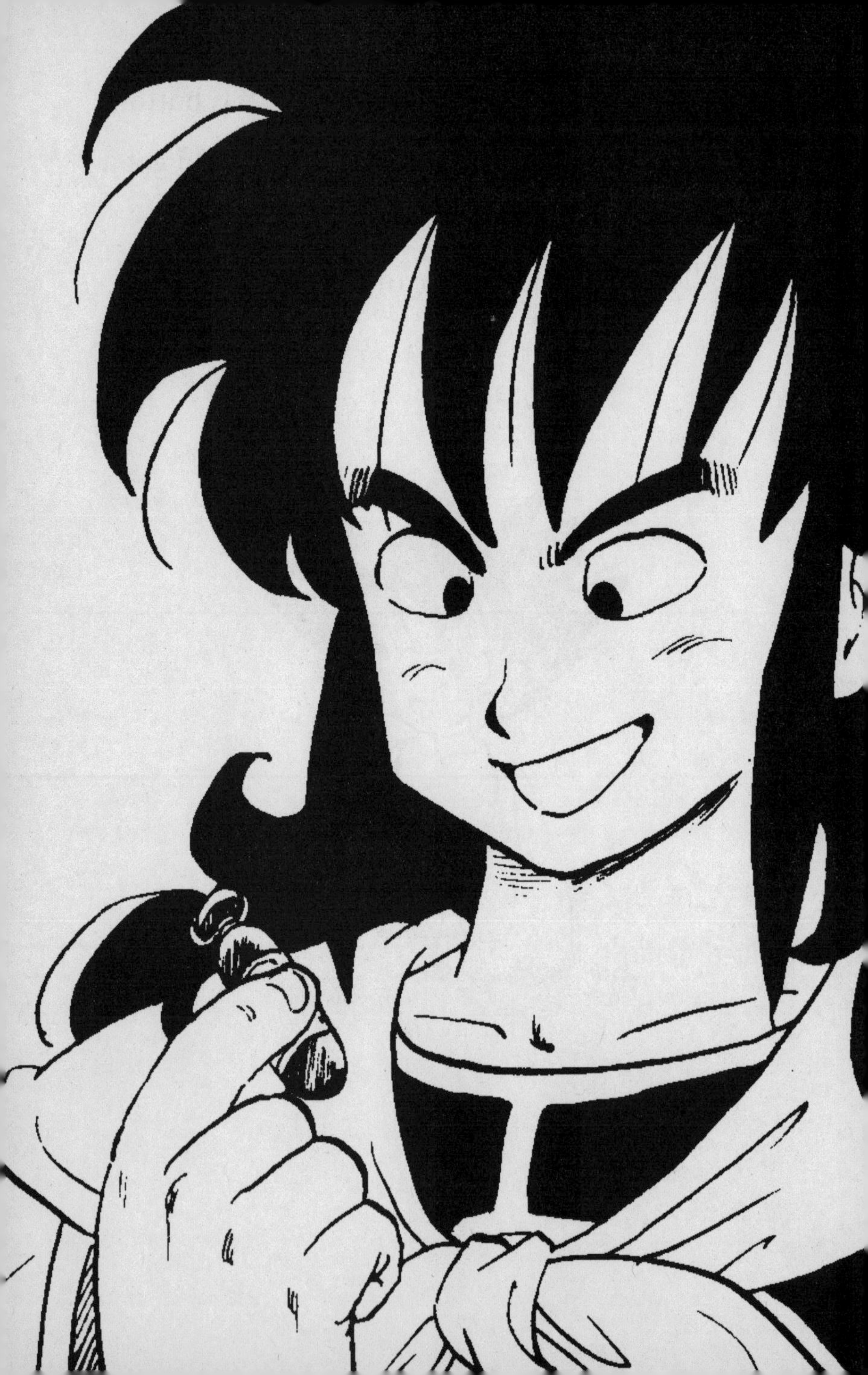

Chapter Eight

HOI

Yamcha tossed a Hoi-Poi pellet into the desert sand. With a POOF it turned into a small jet plane. He turned to Bulma and said with a smile, "Shall we go, Sweetest?"

"Oh brother," Oolong gagged. "This is gonna be a long trip."

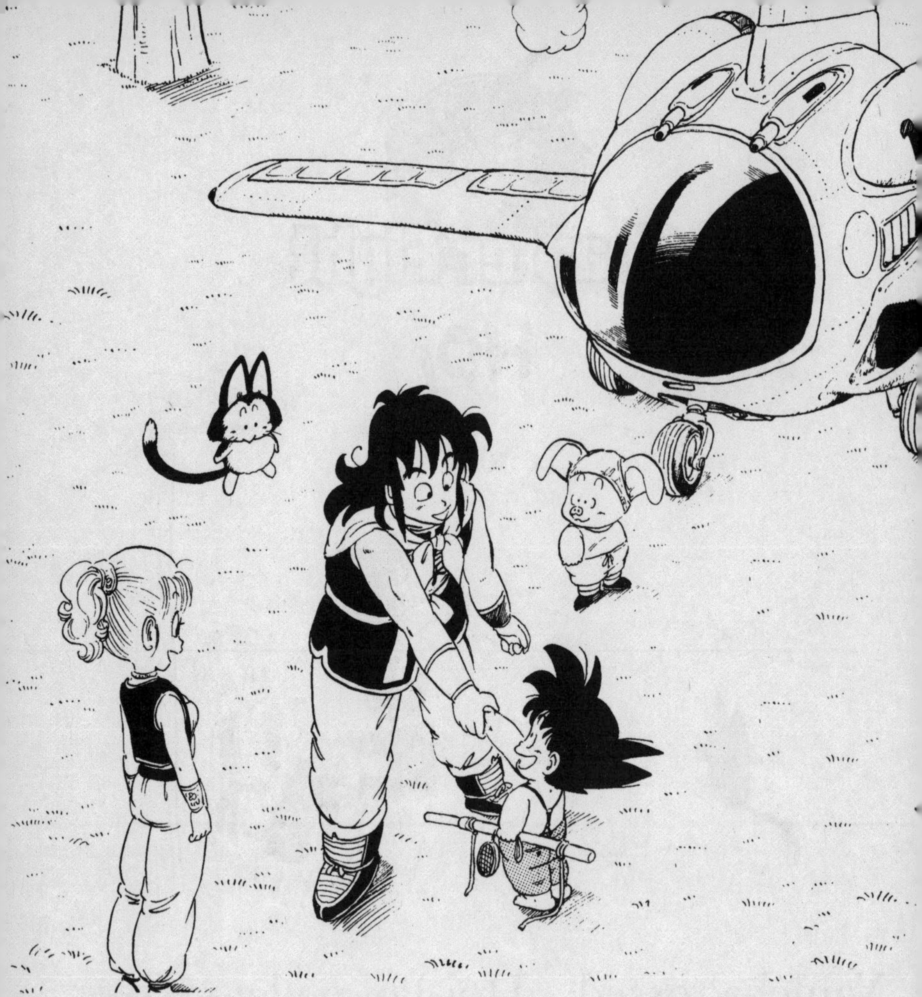

"Goku, I hope you become as powerful as the invincible master Roshi himself," Yamcha said, shaking Goku's hand.

"Me too," Goku nodded. "Well, I guess I'd better get going!

"KINTO'UUUN!" he cried, calling to his magic cloud.

KIN-TO'UUUN !!

Out of nowhere, the enchanted puff zoomed to Goku's side, and he jumped on.

Then Yamcha, Bulma, Pu'ar, and Oolong climbed into the jet. As it rose into the air, Goku hovered nearby on his cloud, waving goodbye to his friends.

"We promise to visit you!" Bulma called.

"All right!" Goku said. "Oolong, Pu'ar, you come too!"

"I'm there!" Pu'ar grinned.

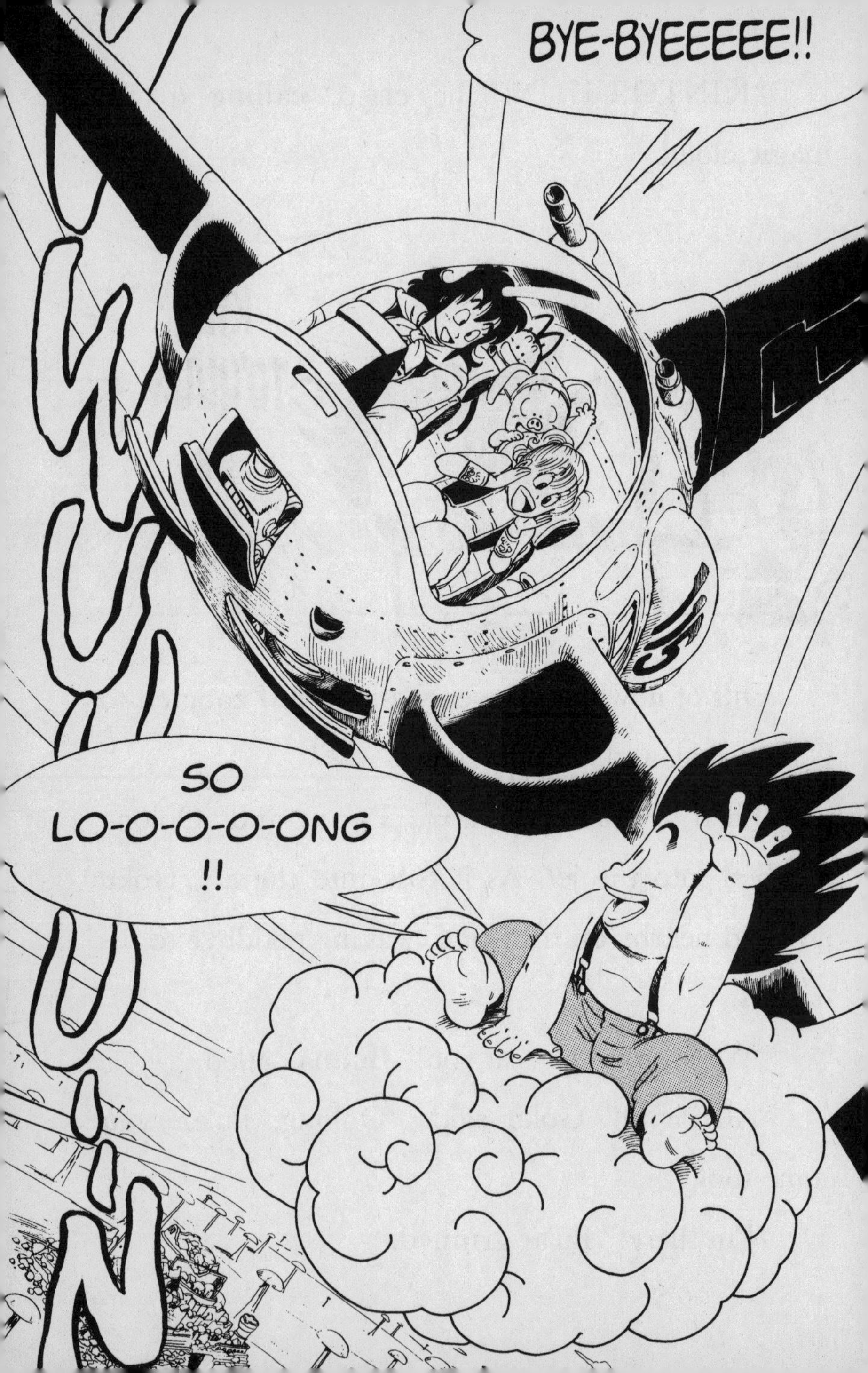
BYE-BYEEEEE!!
SO LO-O-O-O-ONG !!

“Why not?” Oolong said, and his face broke into a grin. “You’re too weird not to want to see again!”

After one final wave Yamcha turned the jet toward the city and Goku shot off in the other direction.

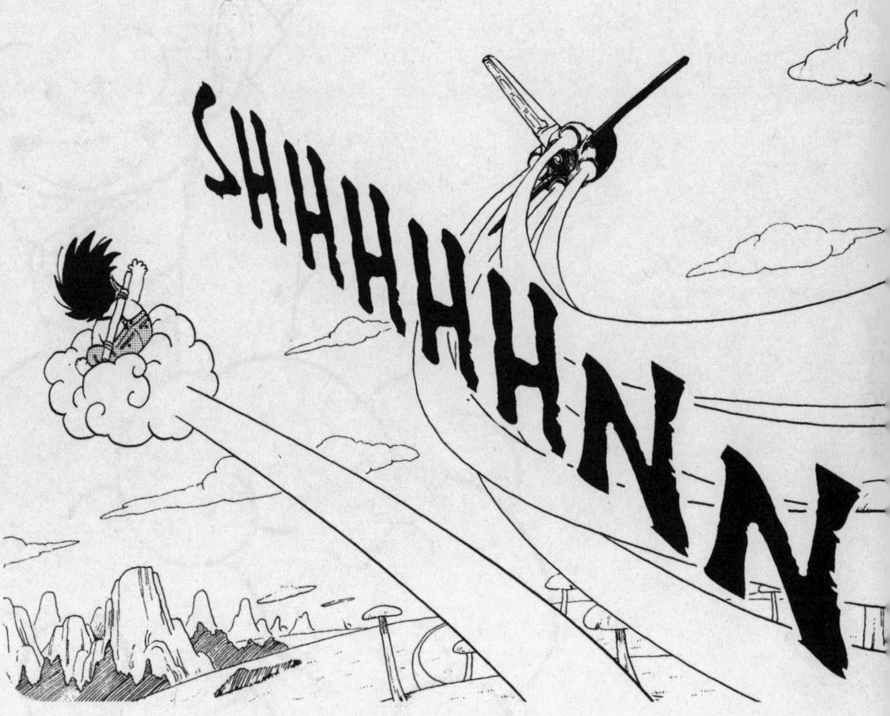
SHHHHHNNN

He zoomed back along the way they had come: out of the desert, over the mushroom forest, and past the now-cool remains of Fry Pan Mountain.

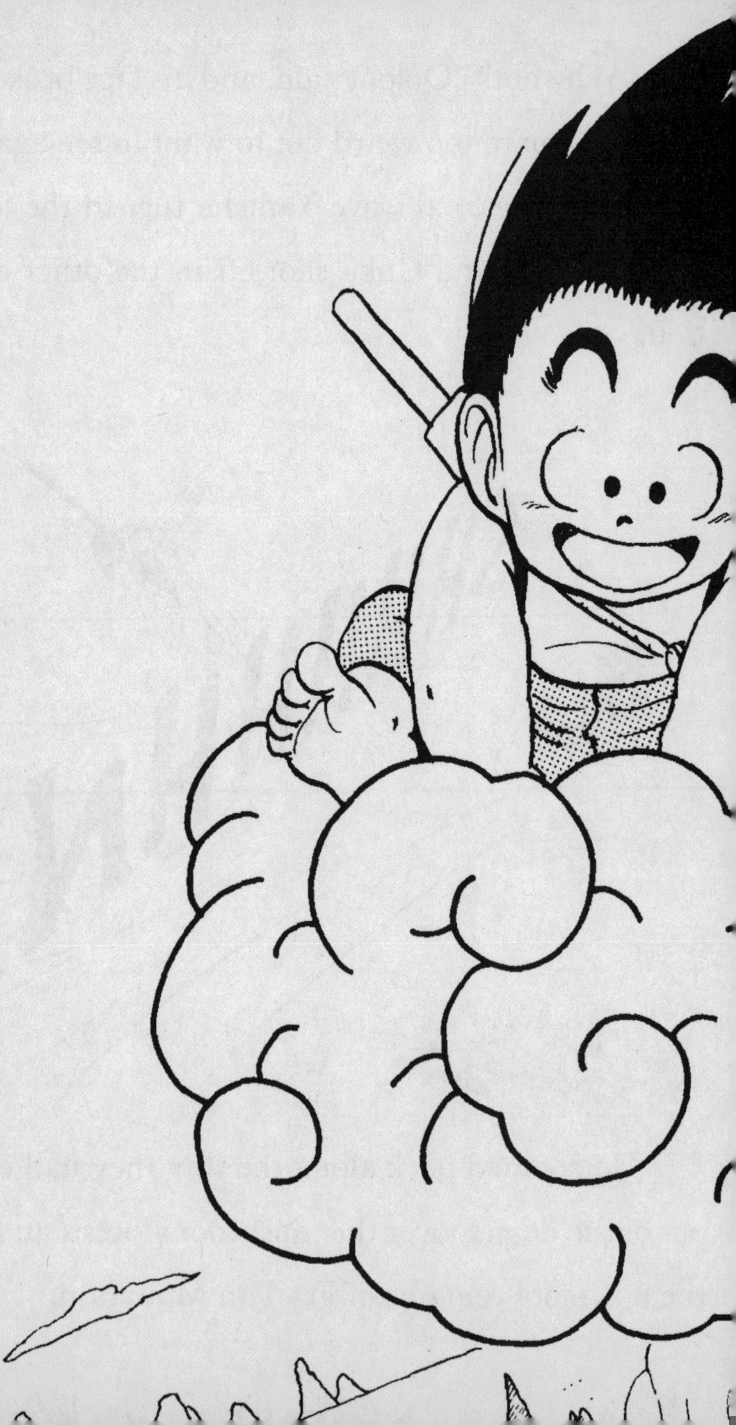

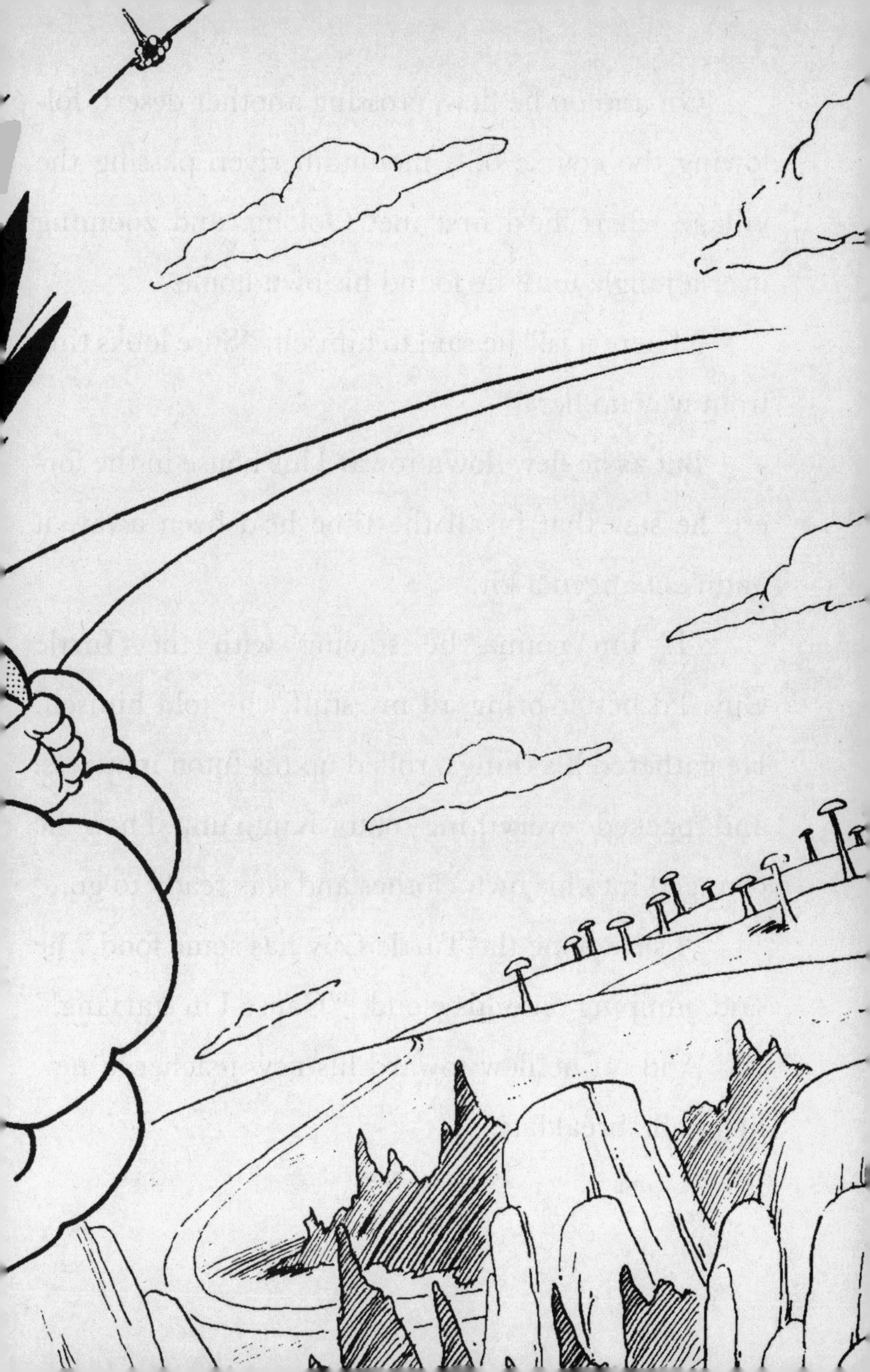

On and on he flew, crossing another desert, following the course of a mountain river, passing the village where he'd first met Oolong, and zooming over a jungle until he found his own home.

"There it is!" he said to himself. "Sure looks tiny from way up here!"

But as he flew down toward his house in the forest, he saw that in all the time he'd been away, it hadn't changed a bit.

"If I'm gonna be staying with the Turtle Guy, I'd better bring all my stuff," he told himself. He gathered his things, rolled up his futon mattress, and packed everything onto Kinto'un. Then he changed into his own clothes and was ready to go.

"I sure hope the Turtle Guy has some food," he said, jumping onto his cloud. "'Cause I'm starving!"

And off he flew toward his new teacher, a new life, and...breakfast.

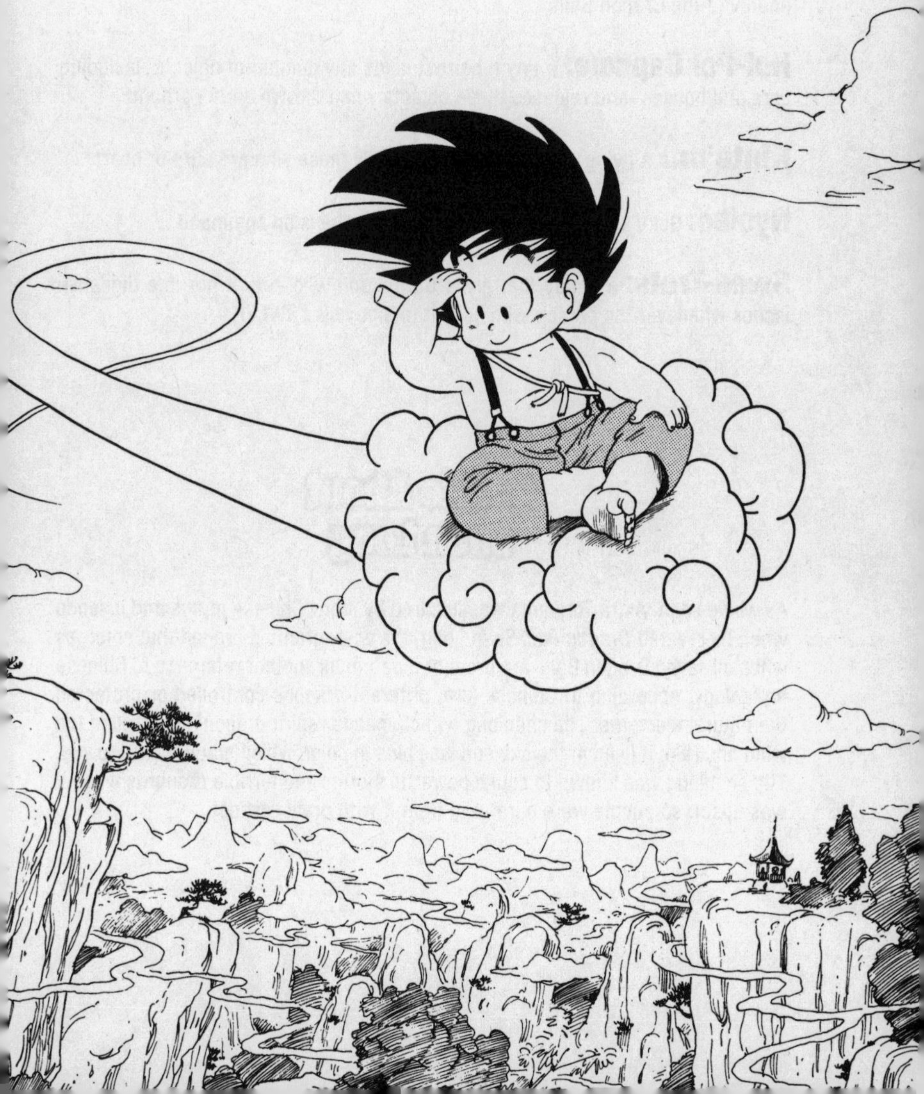

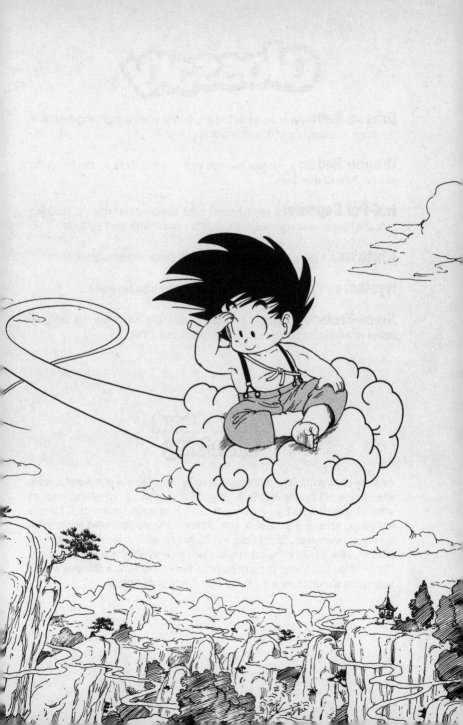

Glossary

Dragon Ball: one of seven mythical orbs that when brought together have the power to summon a wish-granting dragon

Dragon Radar: a machine invented by Bulma that picks up and tracks the energy of the Dragon Balls

Hoi-Poi Capsule: a tiny tube that holds any number of objects—including cars and houses—and releases these objects when thrown on the ground

Kinto'un: a flying cloud that will only carry those who are pure of heart

Nyoibo: Goku's magic fighting staff that lengthens on command

Swee-Trots: a candy that gives the person who eats it horrible digestive issues whenever the person who gave it to him yells "SWEE!"

A Note About Shen Long

As we've seen, Akira Toriyama was inspired by many Chinese myths and legends when he created *Dragon Ball*. Shen Long, the wish-granting dragon that emerges when all seven Dragon Balls are brought together, is another reference to Chinese mythology. According to Chinese lore, different dragons controlled or protected the natural elements. The shenlong (which means "spirit dragon") controlled the wind and rain. It lived in the sky and was blue in color, which made it hard to see. The shenlong was known to cause powerful storms and terrible droughts when it was upset, so people were careful to treat it with great respect.

About the Authors

Akira Toriyama
Original Creator of the *Dragon Ball* Manga

Artist/writer Akira Toriyama burst onto the manga (Japanese comics) scene in 1980, with the wildly popular *Dr. Slump*, a science fiction comedy about the adventures of a mad scientist and his android daughter. In 1984 he created the beloved series *Dragon Ball,* which has been translated into many languages, and, as a series, has sold over 150 million copies in Japan. Toriyama-san lives with his family in Japan.

Gerard Jones
Dragon Ball Chapter Book Author

Gerard Jones has been adapting Japanese manga for English-speaking audiences since 1989, including the entire run of *Dragon Ball* comics for VIZ Media and the *Pokémon* comic strip for Creators Syndicate (reprinted by VIZ as *Pikachu Meets the Press*). He has also written hundreds of original comic books for Marvel, DC, and other publishers, and he is the author of several books on popular culture and children's media, including *Killing Monsters* and the Eisner Award-winning *Men of Tomorrow*. He lives in San Francisco with his wife and son, where he works and teaches at the San Francisco Writers Grotto.

Coming Soon...

Book Six
TRAINING WITH THE MASTER

Now that the Dragon Balls are nothing more than rocks scattered around the globe, what's a young monkey-boy to do? Train with the Turtle Guy, of course! But Goku's not the only one who wants to train with the master, and the new guy is determined to give Goku a run for his money. Find out in the next volume of *Dragon Ball*!

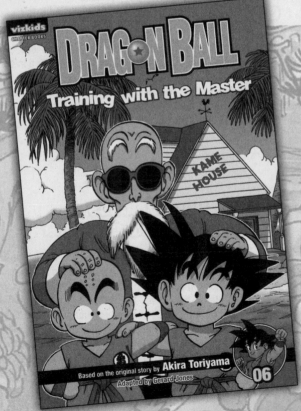

VIZKIDS
CHAPTER BOOKS

DRAGON BALL
Training with the Master

KAME HOUSE

Based on the original story by **Akira Toriyama**
Adapted by **Gerard Jones**

06